Torquere P

This is a work of fiction. Names, characters, places, and incidents either are the product of the author's imagination or are used fictitiously. Any resemblance to actual events, locales, organizations, or persons, living or dead, is entirely coincidental and beyond the intent of either the author or the publisher.

Riding Heartbreak Road
TOP SHELF
An imprint of Torquere Press Publishers
PO Box 2545
Round Rock, TX 78680
Copyright © 2006 by Kiernan Kelly
Cover illustration by Pluto
Published with permission
ISBN: 978-1-934166-25-3 1-934166-25-1
www.torquerepress.com

All rights reserved, which includes the right to reproduce this book or portions thereof in any form whatsoever except as provided by the U.S. Copyright Law. For information address Torquere Press. Inc., PO Box 2545, Round Rock, TX 78680.

First Torquere Press Printing: March 2007
Printed in the USA

If you purchased this book without a cover, you should be aware the this book is stolen property. It was reported as "unsold and destroyed" to the publisher, and neither the author nor the publisher has received any payment for this "stripped book".

Riding Heartbreak Road

Riding Heartbreak Road

Kiernan Kelly

Torquere Press
Inc.
romance for the rest of us
www.torquerepress.com

Riding Heartbreak Road

Chapter One

If there was one fact Jake Goodall was certain of, it was that there was nothing like having 1800 pounds of muscle and fury bucking between his thighs to get his blood boiling and his prick ready to ride more than just a bull.

Providing that his head or his balls weren't flattened like his mother's Sunday morning hotcakes, of course. Eight seconds didn't sound like much time, but when you spent them on the back of a snot-snorting, ass-busting, ball-banging bull as ornery as Wrecking Ball, they could stretch out for years. There was an old saying among bull riders – it wasn't a matter of *if* you got hurt, it was a matter of *when* and *how badly*.

He cleared his mind of everything but the animal beneath him, trying to 'cowboy up' as he strapped his riding hand down under the bull rope and found his seat on the broad back of Wrecking Ball. The bull heaved and banged against the steel side of the bucking chute, seemingly as anxious as Jake to get the show on the road.

Jake's left hand raised high in the air, his right tucked down tightly under the bull rope, his legs clenching Wrecking Ball's sides with the grip of a virgin's ass on prom night, and gave a nod. The gateman flung the chute open and the ride began.

Bucking, jumping, and twisting, the bull came alive under Jake's ass as it burst into the arena. It was like trying to ride a tornado but he managed to stay over his hand, keeping his seat for the full time. The whistle blew and he vaulted off the bull's back, landing squarely on his rump in the dark brown sawdust of the arena.

Jake was up and running before Wrecking Ball even realized he was gone, and the rodeo clowns ran interference as Jake sprinted to the fence, getting away with his hide slightly dented, but still intact. Swatting the dust from the seat of his jeans with his hat, he grinned as his score was announced. Thirty-seven points for him and another forty for the bull meant that he'd made the finals, and he was still smiling as he worked his way out of the arena after collecting his bull rope and black Stetson, heading toward the back pens. He stopped only long enough to pick up his gray duffle bag, slinging the strap over his shoulder. He'd be back tomorrow afternoon for the short-go, and a shot at the prize money and the buckle.

Stripping off his riding glove, he flexed his fingers, then unbuckled his chaps and stuffed them, his glove, his protective vest, and his bull rope into his duffle bag. Picking it up, he headed out toward the parking lot where his beat-to-shit pickup waited, next to the carnival midway. The county fair was still in full swing at this hour, tinny music blaring and colorful lights twinkling in the dark as the locals screamed and laughed, riding the Ferris wheel or throwing baseballs at wooden bottles on the midway in hopes of winning a stuffed bear.

The girls were there as they always were, the buckle bunnies, clustered outside the gate waiting for the riders as they left the arena. They batted their eyes at Jake, smiling and giggling, drawn by his youthful good looks and well-muscled body, packed as it was into his tight blue chambray shirt and worn jeans. He tipped his hat and smiled his boyish, lop-sided grin right back at them, but kept walking. He didn't have any interest in them, though he kept that fact to himself.

On his way to his truck, parked amid shiny horse trailers and motor homes, he nodded amicably at several riders and rodeo hands, but he didn't stop to hold a conversation with any of them. Jake didn't keep any close friends on the local circuit. Most of them were friendly enough folk - the riders especially having a great deal in common with him, and he'd spent his share of nights swapping war stories with them over longnecks - but he didn't try to forge friendships with any of them. First of all, they were the competition, pure and simple. He didn't travel much and had no need of a traveling partner, a fellow rider and friend to share expenses. Secondly, more than a few of the local cowboys were notoriously short-tempered with men who preferred a cock to a hen, and friends had a way of finding out about things like that. When he was in the company of other riders, he talked the talk and they had never realized that he didn't walk the walk.

In fact, letting folks in general know about his preferences could prove to be downright unhealthy in Jake's neck of the woods. There was always a chance that he would find himself at the bottom of a bullpen getting danced on by a ton of pissed off prime rib, or tied to the back bumper of a pickup doing sixty down some godforsaken back road. Even his family and his friends, the ones he'd grown up with, didn't know which side of the fence he rode. He'd even gone so far as to have girlfriends from time to time, especially when he was younger and on the verge of figuring things out, although for obvious reasons none of them had lasted long and were mostly just for show. Not that he hadn't dipped his wick now and then… but those times were few and far between and only out of sheer desperation.

He'd fought the truth about himself for the longest time but in the end he'd come to privately accept himself, although his iron-hard fists still spoke loud and clear to the contrary on the rare occasions when some liquored-up lunkhead had the poor sense to call him on it.

The simple truth was that he liked men. Period. Even the few women he'd dated had been as flat as the earth before Columbus. Big breasts had always turned him off – they just seemed to get in the way of things, as far as Jake was concerned. He was never quite sure what he was supposed to be doing with them, anyway. Plus, there was just something about iron muscles and hard dicks that got his britches to tenting.

All this he kept to himself, going about his business. When his physical needs got to be too much for him to bear, he'd travel to towns well away from West Fork - sometimes as far as Dallas - in order to find companionship. He was used to it. It was just the way things were.

Could be that he'd find that folks were more tolerant in the big-time, on the pro-circuit where the boys rode bulls for more money in one purse than Jake had yet ever seen together in one spot in his whole lifetime, but he hadn't gotten that far yet in his career. He was still riding in local county fairs and rodeos, where the entry fee wasn't more than he could make in a week selling galvanized buckets and pre-cut fence posts down at his daddy's feed store.

Reaching his pickup, an old clunker held together by not much more than a spit and a prayer and a roll of duct tape, Jake threw his duffle bag onto the seat, and then slid his solid frame behind the wheel. Starting her up, he headed out with a particular destination in mind.

Whether it was the thrill of the ride or the knowledge that he was still in the running for the prize money, Jake found himself the proud owner of a raging hard-on and was of a mind to do something about it. He'd take his chances at the Lobo over in Stillwater where, if he were lucky he'd find somebody like-minded – or at least drunk enough not to care - or else get shit-faced on shots of rotgut and probably spend the night in the bed of his pickup, jerking off under the stars.

He hoped for the first, but was used to the second. Wouldn't be the first time he'd had to whack his own weed and it likely wouldn't be the last. Still, the night was young and so was he, and he'd see what was what when he got there.

***

Brent Miller was royally pissed off. He'd just driven nearly 1500 miles in two days and was close enough to Dallas to practically *smell* the money he was going to make by signing the new account he'd spent the last six months stroking, only to have his BMW break down in a godforsaken spit of a town in the middle of nowhere.

He'd been certain that he'd found a short-cut on the creased and coffee-splattered road-map, but after a few hours of twisting and turning roads had instead found himself driving down a patch of tarmac that was not much better than a cattle trail, swerving to avoid potholes big enough to swallow a Caddy. The road had become so bad that for the last ten minutes he'd been cursing himself for his foolish fear of flying. He could have been happily ensconced in his luxury hotel room in Dallas well before now, enjoying a frozen something-or-other and the view of the Dallas skyline instead of battering his balls on this road to hell.

Just when he'd been ready to turn around and try to find his way back to Interstate 30, the car had shuddered violently, banging and bucking under his ass. Luckily for Brent, his BMW held it together just long enough to coast to a stop on the main drag of the tiny hamlet of Stillwater, Texas, and not in the middle of the miles of desolate road between there and the Interstate or he'd have been screwed for certain.

He had decided that he might be able to fit the entire town of Stillwater inside Radio City Music Hall and still have plenty of room left over for parking. The whole of the main street – it was actually dubbed "*Broadway*," a comically pretentious name for the potholed and cracked strip of single-lane blacktop that it was – consisted of a small diner, a barbershop with an honest-to-Christ red and white striped revolving barber pole outside the door, a dry goods store, a bar, and a single pump gas station with one mechanics' bay. Back behind the main drag Brent could see a few rows of gray-shingled, weather-beaten houses, most with bright white sheets and colorful quilts flapping on clotheslines strung across the yard. Beyond them for as far as the eye could see stretched the rest of Texas.

Brent missed the city already, even though he'd only been gone for a few days. He missed the hustle and bustle, the noise and the night-life, but most of all he missed the *comforts*. He missed being able to walk down to the corner to grab a frothy cappuccino, sitting at a side-walk table and perusing the *Times* or the *Journal*. He missed cable television, pay-per-view, the Internet, gay bars, Bloomingdales, and Chinese takeout.

Brent shook his head and folded his arms across his chest, sighing forlornly as he stared down at the legs of the mechanic who was clanking and clinking something underneath the body of the BMW. From the looks of this town, he might well be missing indoor plumbing before long, as well.

The local mechanic, a grizzled old man in oil-stained overalls, rolled himself out from under Brent's Beamer, wiping his hands on a rag so black with grime that it made his gnarled, arthritic fingers even dirtier. In a phlegmy voice he told Brent that his CV joint was "shot to shit and back again," emphasizing the finality of his diagnosis by hocking a wad of snot into the dirt.

Needless to say, the mechanic didn't carry BMW parts in his shop, which doubled as a convenience store of sorts (signs stuck up at haphazard angles on the dirt-streaked window promised "boiled peanuts, Red Man Chewing Tobacco, and LoneStar beer), and informed Brent that it would take at least two days to get the part that he needed in from the distributor in Dallas. Plus, it would take at least another day to install it. That, the old man went on to say, was providing that Billy Joe Flynt - the one man, evidently, in all of Stillwater who knew anything about "them foreign jobs," as the mechanic referred to Brent's BMW - was back from fishing over on the Neches.

Finding that he had no choice in the matter, Brent left his car at the station and, having received directions from the old man – which included such colorful directives as "Past the rock what looks like two titties" – headed out on foot to find a room.

The only motel within walking distance was the picturesque Stillwater Inn, a square, squat stucco box that sat like a white Lego-block on the very outskirts of town. By the time Brent reached it, he was soaked with sweat, and his temper had gotten decidedly worse for the walk. His room was a single, decorated with horrid orange drapes, a cow-hide bedspread, and three faded prints of cow-boys on horseback tacked to the wall. It

boasted an air conditioner that clanged and
clattered and blew worse than a ten-dollar
whore, and a television set that was bolted to
the dresser and received all of three channels –
if the weather was clear and the wind was
blowing right. He was almost surprised to find
that it included a tiny, rust-spotted bathroom
instead of an outhouse in the parking lot.

Showering under a dribble of tepid water
that seemed all the lime-encrusted showerhead
could manage to spit out, he sat on the bed and
waited until the sun went down before leaving
his room again. He passed the time watching
an episode of *Bonanza* that was so snowy that
Brent was forced to squint to tell the difference
between Hoss and Hop Sing.

Heading into town – once again passing
the infamous Tittie Rock - he stopped to grab a
bite to eat at the town's only diner, *Ma Mabel's Country Kitchen*. Sliding onto the
squeaky red vinyl seat of a booth, he perused
the single page, hand-typed menu while his
pony-tailed waitress, Bobbie, stood tableside,
all but shoving her tits in his face and popping
her chewing gum. His choices were meatloaf,
hamburgers, and something called chicken-
fried chicken.

He ordered the meatloaf, which turned out
to be thick-cut and spicy and drenched with
rich brown gravy. It was surprisingly good
and, along with the tall glass of sweet tea he'd
ordered with his meal, put Brent in a better

mood than he'd been in all afternoon.

He turned down an offer from Bobbie to meet her after her shift, gave her a ten-dollar tip on a nine-dollar tab simply to see the look on her face, and left Ma Mabel's fine dining establishment, strolling slowly down Broadway.

Sitting at a round, wooden table in the town's only bar, Brent nursed a rock glass of J&B and wondered what in the blue hell he was supposed to do with himself for the next three days besides gaining fifty pounds eating at Ma Mabel's and fighting off Bobbie-the-waitress.

As the evening lengthened, the bar began to fill up with men and women in cowboy hats and boots, their scuffed boot heels tapping on the hardwood floor. Brent watched the men surreptitiously, eyeing their asses and crotches that were stuffed into their tight Levis, wondering if any of them might be amenable to spending a couple of hours squeaking the mattress with a stranded businessman.

The locals eyed him curiously and not a few suspiciously, one or two giving him a curt nod as they passed his table. He got the distinct impression that a couple of them wanted to ask him straight up if he was gay, and not because they were interested in getting into his pants.

To a one they looked like hard asses and as straight as two-by-fours - much to Brent's disappointment - and far more interested in flirting with the big-haired women in boot-cut Levis and fringed cowgirl shirts than in a stranger who set off their gay radar. He contented himself with silently admiring the cowboys' muscular frames over the rim of his glass, even though his cock strained at the zipper of his chinos as a result.

***

It was well past ten o'clock by the time Jake's pickup crunched onto the gravel of the crowded parking lot of the Lobo, lucky to find a single spot empty around the back of the building. It was Saturday night and the boys were out in force, all looking for a barstool and a beer and a little pussy after a hard week's worth of work on the ranch. He pulled in, threw the truck in park and turned off the engine, which sputtered and groaned – whether in defiance or relief, Jake couldn't tell – before falling silent, and then pocketed his keys.

Walking into the bar, Jake looked around for familiar faces. Finding none - which was fine with him considering his motive for being there in the first place - he ambled over to the bar and asked for a longneck. Since the barstools and tables were all full, he found a relatively empty spot near the jukebox and leaned back against a wall behind the pool table. He crossed one foot over the other and idly watched a couple of wranglers rack and stack the balls. His eyes drifted over the room as he took a long swallow of his beer, pausing when he spotted a man sitting alone at a table near the back of the room.

Jake knew immediately that the man was not a local simply by the way he was dressed. The cowboys and ranchers who scratched out a living in these parts didn't go out to grab a brew on a Saturday night duded up like an undertaker. The man wore an immaculate white dress shirt and a pair of pressed khaki pants, and Jake could see spit-polished dress shoes under the table and a dark blue suit jacket hung neatly over the back of his chair.

The man was the prettiest thing in the bar, in Jake's opinion. The stranger had thick blue-black hair, spiked and tousled, and a clean-shaven square jaw. Smooth dark brows shadowed eyes that looked to be the color of melted chocolate, from where Jake stood. The stranger's shoulders looked broad and strong under his pristine white shirt, and his fingers were long and slender as they raised a glass to his full lips. Lips, Jake thought, that made a man want to do some kissing, among other things.

Jake decided to take his chances on striking up a conversation with the stranger. At worst, he'd end up spending some time talking to somebody from somewhere other than this godforsaken, dust-blown part of Texas; at best, if he was lucky, he might not have to spend the night pulling on his pecker all by his lonesome. Pushing off the wall, he threaded his way through the crowd toward the table at the back of the room.

"Howdy," Jake said, giving the man a quick nod.

"Hi," Brent answered, looking up in surprise.

Jake looked him over, thinking that they could be exact opposites; him lanky and tall with fair hair, sun-browned and a thick drawl, and the man sitting at the table with pale skin and sleek dark hair and a precise, clipped accent.

Jake glanced down with a questioning look toward an empty chair at the stranger's table, and the man responded with a graceful wave of his manicured hand. Sitting himself down in the wooden captain's chair, Jake placed his bottle on the table, and settled back, stretching his legs out. He spent a few moments looking everywhere but at the man sitting across from him.

"You're new around here, ain't you? Visiting kin?" Jake finally asked, his fingers absently picking at the label on his beer bottle.

"No," Brent replied, shaking his head, his own fingers running circles around the rim of his rock glass. "My car broke down a little ways out. Barely made it here, then quit altogether. The mechanic tells me it was the CV joint."

"Yup, them roads out there'll do it every time unless you're driving something solid like a Ram, and even then it's a gamble. I'm Jake Goodall, by the way," Jake said, sticking out his hand over the table.

Brent took Jake's hand in a firm grip. "Nice to meet you, Jake. I'm Brent Miller." Jake knew that he'd hung on to Brent's hand for just a heartbeat or two longer than necessary. "Nice little town you have here."

"I guess. Ain't much, though. A man could spit a wad bigger and more interesting than this town. I'm not from Stillwater. I'm from a couple of towns over in West Fork, but all the towns 'round here are near the same. You been to Dallas? Now, that there is a *city*," Jake said before taking a swig of beer.

Brent's hand had been warm and soft in his, not like the calloused, rough paws of the few ranch hands he'd managed to bed. He liked the way it had felt and hadn't wanted to let it go.

"I was on my way to Dallas when my car broke down."

"That a fact? What in hell made you get off I-30, then? Ain't nothing out this way but cowpies and sagebrush. You missed Dallas altogether!"

Brent rolled his eyes and snorted in agreement. "I thought I found a shortcut."

"You thought wrong."

The two men chuckled a bit in that polite

way strangers have when they laugh together, each looking down at his drink. Falling into silence, they let the laughter and music of the bar fill the space between them for a few moments.

"So, what do you do for a living, Jake? I'm into computers, myself - high-end, cutting-edge software. I own the business, actually," Brent said, obviously trying to stir up a conversation. "That's why I was going to Dallas. I have a new account to sign."

"I work down at my old man's feed store most times, and I rodeo on the weekends. Bull riding."

"You're a bull rider? Isn't that dangerous?" Brent cringed when the words left his mouth. Jake smiled a little at Brent's discomfort.

"Yeah, I suppose it is, now and then. I've seen a lot of good riders get beat to hell. They'd have a bad wreck and get freight-trained – that's when you get run over by the bull," Jake explained, ignoring the slight tremor that ran across Brent's shoulders. "It ain't pretty, and that's the goddamn truth. Took a few bad tumbles myself. Broke my riding arm once and two ribs another time. But when you get the itch to ride, the only solution is to scratch it or go crazy. Matter of fact, I rode today and made the finals. Going to ride again tomorrow, maybe take home the buckle and some money."

"Wow, that's great. The finals, huh? That

sounds fascinating." Brent smiled. "I suppose you get to travel a lot then, huh?"

"Nah… only the pro-circuit riders travel much. The rest of us have to work for a living. A man needs a fistful of money to ride in the pros."

Brent nodded his understanding, and looked down at Jake's fingers nervously picking at the label of his beer bottle. He gave Jake a frank look. "What are you doing here alone on a Saturday night? A cowboy like you must have a girlfriend. Is she going to meet you here later?" he asked, his dark brown eyes searching the cowboy's face as if looking for an answer.

Jake shook his head, unwilling to meet Brent's eyes. "No, I ain't meetin' nobody tonight. Don't have anybody special, truth be told. Too busy working and riding for that."

Brent fell silent for a moment.

"Well, in my opinion, you're not missing anything. I don't find girls all that interesting anyway," Brent said softly, watching Jake's face. "Never had much use for them, myself. They're just not my thing, if you know what I mean."

"Yeah?" Jake answered as he flicked his blue eyes up to meet Brent's brown ones briefly, before suddenly finding the label of his LoneStar once again irresistibly interesting. If he was hearing what he thought he was hearing, then perhaps things would be getting a lot

more interesting in Stillwater for Mr. Brent
Miller of New York City.

After a moment he gave his shoulder a
slight shake and whispered, "Yeah, me, too, I
reckon."

Brent's face showed a small, secret smile.
"I'd guess that must be a pretty hard row to
hoe around here," Brent said, looking around
pointedly at the rough crowd that filled the bar.
"Lonely sometimes, I suppose. Same thing
when you're out on the road a lot, like I am."

"I suppose," Jake agreed, finally looking
up, meeting and holding Brent's sympathetic
gaze. He felt a familiar tickle in his groin, and
tried hard to keep from grinning. It was looking like he wasn't going to have to be spending
the night alone in the bed of his pickup after
all. "You ever watch bull riding, Brent?" he
asked impulsively, using the man's name for
the first time.

"No, I can't say that I have. I do remember
my dad taking me to a rodeo in Madison
Square Garden once when I was about eight or
nine years old, but I don't remember much
about it," Brent confessed. Then he added,
"but I'd like to sometime, Jake. It sounds exciting."

"If you have to wait on your car anyway,
you're welcome to come watch me ride tomorrow," Jake said, giving a shrug of his shoulders, as if he really didn't care if Brent came or
not, although nothing was further from the

truth. "I can pick you up in the morning. Or you can save me the trip and come back with me tonight. I know a real nice place where we can camp out the night, if you'd like." Jake held his breath, waiting for Brent's answer.

"Camp out?" Brent repeated.

Jake waited for Brent to figure it out; that Jake would not want to come back to Brent's seedy motel room in a town the size of Stillwater. Two men sleeping in the same room with one bed in it would be no less discreet than erecting a fifty-foot billboard with a big flashing red arrow pointing to his room that said "GAY COWBOY HERE." If Jake intended to get up close and personal with Brent they'd need to find somewhere private, and in this stretch of the barren, wild and wooly west that meant camping out somewhere on the prairie.

"Sure, I'd like that. Haven't been camping since I was a boy, either," Brent replied.

Jake nodded his head and took another swallow of LoneStar to mask the grin that was threatening to crease his face. "I have a pup tent and a sleeping bag in my truck. Figure that's pretty much all we'll be needing," he said, meeting Brent's eyes again and holding his gaze this time, eliminating any doubt about how they were going to spend the long hours of the night.

Chapter Two

They made two stops in Jake's old pickup before heading out toward the place Jake had in mind for them to make camp. The first was at Bill's Texaco, where Jake ran in and bought a few staples and two sixes of LoneStar from the same shriveled and grayed mechanic who'd given Brent the bad news about his Beamer; and the second was the motel, where it was Brent's turn to run in. He returned from his room a moment later with a small over-night bag that contained his toiletries.

The drive took a little over an hour, much of which was spent traveling over rough, un-marked dirt roads that only someone who'd been born and bred in the area would know about. The pickup bounced and banged its way along, jarring Jake's spine and making him feel as though he were riding on the bare, sharp springs of the seats, rather than on the cracked and scarred leather. The ride got even worse and he threw the truck into four-wheel drive and took it off-roading over the rough prairie. Jake breathed a sigh of relief when he pulled the truck up and parked under a copse of pine near the bank of a river, and he could hear Brent doing the same.

Jake set about setting up the tent and gathering the makings for a fire, while Brent stood watching him, occasionally trying to be helpful but not succeeding. Jake gave him a look and finally just stepped back out of his way, shifting from one foot to the other, his hands shoved in his pockets.

While he tried not to chuckle at the city slicker's helplessness, Jake found that he liked the way Brent was looking at him, as if Jake were some kind of survival expert. In truth, all Jake was doing was pitching a pup tent and kindling a small fire that any ten-year-old Boy Scout could have banged out easily, but the expression on Brent's face made it clear that to him it seemed no less complicated than brain surgery.

After the fire had been firmly established, Jake stood up and stretched to his full length, working out a few kinks that had been plaguing his back since his ride that afternoon. "I'm going to take a bath; I still reek of bullshit," he said with a laugh. "You coming?"

Wordlessly, Brent nodded, and trailed Jake toward the bank of the lazily flowing river. He stood back again, watching Jake unselfconsciously strip and run out into the water, flinging himself into the cold depths of the river with a whooping holler. Jake came up sputtering and shaking his blond head, flinging droplets of water in every direction.

"Well? Are you coming? I'm a-waitin'!"
he called out to Brent from the water.

Brent nodded, and began to unbutton his
shirt. Maybe it was the booze or maybe it was
the moonlight but Brent hurried as he pulled
off his shirt, kicked off his shoes, and went to
work on his pants.

***

Brent thought that Jake was quite possibly
the most beautiful man he had ever seen naked. Every ropy muscle in the cowboy's toned
body had stood out in stark relief where the
pale silver moonlight had kissed them. Brent
had also been given a good look at Jake's
package before he had dived into the water,
and had not been disappointed in what he'd
seen. Thick and uncut, Jake's penis had hung
heavily between his legs, framed by a dark triangle of curls and a pair of strong, pale thighs.

Naked, Brent pulled off his socks and
tucked them into his shoes. Stepping to the
river's edge, he toed the water hesitantly,
jumping back and swearing softly at the freezing temperature.

"Best to just throw yourself in," Jake called
as he treaded water about ten yards out from
the bank. "It's a mite cold, but I expect that
you'll get used to it fast enough." Brent could
tell that Jake wasn't really in all that much of a
hurry for him to get into the water. His eyes

were trained on Brent's groin, like he was trying to imagine what the man's penis would look like when it was fully erect.

Nodding, Brent took a deep breath and followed Jake's lead, running and hurling himself into the river.

It was like diving into a pitcher of ice water.

Brent went under, the freezing temperature of the river shocking his system and making his body feel as though an icy vise were crushing his chest. Breaking through the surface, he bellowed and gasped for air. He went down again, his limbs numbing and having a hard time keeping him afloat in the ice-cold water. His head broke the water a second time, his stiffening arms banging on the water's surface and his legs kicking, trying to tread water.

A strong arm wrapped itself around his shoulders and kept his head above water, pulling Brent back toward the shore. In a few moments, he found himself out of the water and on the grassy bank, curling up into a shivering ball.

Jake pulled him up from the ground and helped him stumble back to the campsite. He wrapped a threadbare, scratchy plaid blanket around Brent's shoulders, and pushed him down near the fire. Jake squatted down, poking at the burning logs with a stick and sending the flames higher and sparks swirling up with the smoke. He scooted over, sitting behind Brent and pulling the shuddering man back against his chest, rubbing his hands over the thin blanket that covered Brent's arms.

"You city boys ain't got no blood, you know that?" He laughed softly, as Brent's trembling began to subside in the face of the warmth of the fire and Jake's body heat.

"You c-country boys must be made of s-steel," Brent mumbled in reply. He was mortified that he'd been unable to tolerate the temperature of the water of the river, and could feel his face burning with more than the heat of the flames. This trip was turning out to be a disaster. First, he'd let his ignorance show clearly in his clueless behavior when Jake had set the camp up, and now this. He half-turned in Jake's arms, looking at the cowboy. "How do you do it? That water was f-freezing!"

"I expect that I'm just used to it, is all." Jake smiled and let his eyes wander over Brent's face, reaching up and hesitantly passing his thumb lightly over Brent's trembling lips. "I'm really sorry. I shouldn't have made you jump in like that. I should've known better. Look at you... Your lips are near blue," he whispered, "Got to warm them up." Jake leaned in a bit and he brushed his warm lips over Brent's cold ones. Pulling back, he looked into Brent's dark eyes, waiting to see the reaction to his kiss.

"Warm is good," Brent answered softly. He leaned in closer to Jake; his body angled for more contact. Their kiss was longer this time, firmer.

Brent lost himself in Jake's arms, in the feeling of hard muscles pressing almost painfully around him and the softness of the lips kissing him. In the back of his mind a small voice questioned how a simple kiss could possibly wreak such havoc with his body and cause his heart to thump faster and faster. His groin tightened as the rising heat of Jake's body pulled a likewise reaction from him.

In the quiet of the night, the soft wet sounds of their lips pushing and pulling against one another's vied with the crackling of the fire, the chirping of cicadas, and the gentle lapping of the water against the riverbank. Across the black blanket of the sky, the moon shone and a million stars glittered, silent witnesses to the two hard, muscular bodies that sat entwined far below them.

Twisting until he was able to reach up and thread his fingers through the tousled, wet strands of Jake's hair, Brent pulled him closer, deepening their kiss. Parting his lips, he flicked his tongue along Jake's lower lip and was rewarded by Jake's tongue meeting his own.

Brent felt himself pushed backwards until he lay flush against the hard ground, borne down by Jake's weight. Propping himself up on one elbow alongside of him, Jake's free hand cupped the side of Brent's face as their tongues wrestled with one another, both fighting for dominance and neither one winning. Brent's arms slipped out from under the blanket, and he ran his hands up and down over Jake's arms, kneading his strong biceps. Suddenly, Jake broke away, looking down at Brent through half-hooded eyes.

Carefully, slowly, like a child opening a beautifully wrapped gift, Jake peeled back the frayed plaid blanket, exposing the rest of Brent's skin to the cool night air. His blue eyes drifted over Brent's body, followed closely by Jake's fingers trailing after them with a feather-soft touch.

Brent's skin tingled under Jake's fingertips, gooseflesh raised by more than just his recent chill. His body undulated as the gentle touches sent his lust-level soaring into the outer stratosphere.

Jake sighed, his eyes on the body of the man lying next to him, his olive skin cast in orange by the flickering light of the campfire. Brent knew he looked good, his body toned and sculpted by virtue of time spent in the gym, his chest, belly, and legs thickly dusted with soft dark hair. Between his thighs, Brent's erection bobbed with his growing need, the purpling head looking smooth and rounded without a covering of foreskin and already leaking a few drops of pearly fluid.

A calloused thumb brushed against a dark nipple, teasing the tiny nub into stiffness before Jake lowered his head and drew it into his warm, wet mouth, swirling his tongue over it, teasing it between his teeth.

Brent arched into Jake's mouth, one hand still fisted in his damp hair. The chilled night air felt even colder when Jake released his mouth-warmed nipple to it, reclaiming Brent's lips in another hard and eager kiss.

Jake's fingers slid down over the flat plane of Brent's belly, smoothing over sharp hip-bones and thick black pubic hair, until they brushed against the hot velvet skin of Brent's erection. Breaking their kiss again, Jake whispered hoarsely, "Is this what you want?"

"What I *need*," Brent answered breathlessly, his hands sliding over Jake's shoulders, pushing down and urging him on.

Brent's pelvis tilted up into his hand as Jake wrapped his fingers around the solid length. The heat of Jake's mouth heated Brent's skin as Jake lowered his face to hover over Brent's cock, ghosting his breath over the rounded head.

Brent made a choked noise as Jake flicked his tongue out, licking lightly across the crown. Brent twisted his hand tightly in Jake's hair; Jake grunted and swirled his tongue under the head's ridge, then nipped his way carefully and lightly down along the length and back again. Jake opened his mouth he drew in as much of it as he could, sucking hard at the tender flesh. Brent's gasped and moaned, thrusting upward into Jake's mouth.

Jake released Brent's hot length only long enough to wet his fingers, brushing them over Brent's sac and sliding them between the his quivering thighs until they reached the small puckered opening that lay there. Rubbing it gently as he sucked fiercely on Brent's cock, he waited only a moment before slipping his finger past the clenching ring of muscle and deep into Brent's ass.

Brent moaned louder than before as Jake's finger invaded his body, and he held on tighter, pushing up into the hot wet cavern of Jake's mouth. His moan was one of bitter disappointment when Jake released his cock and pulled his finger out of his asshole, ignoring Brent's irritated grunt.

Jake's blue eyes were nearly black with lust as they looked into Brent's own. "I'm going to ride you now, boy. I'm going to sink myself up to my hips in you. Right now," he muttered, roughly pushing Brent over onto his stomach and pulling his hips up until Brent was on his hands and knees. He quickly positioned himself between Brent's legs, rubbing his cock teasingly over Brent's lower back.

Brent looked back over his shoulder at Jake, his lips parted in excitement. "My bag…by the tent. It has…"

"We don't need anything but what nature gave us," Jake growled. He grunted but paused, not wanting to stop but knowing that

Brent was right. He dashed to the tent, and came back with a tube of Astroglide and a condom.

"Hurry!" Brent called out, his voice strained with need.

***

Jake returned from the tent in seconds, already tearing the condom package open with his teeth but stopped dead in his tracks as he looked at Brent and saw him as if for the first time.

Backlit by the flames and touched by the moonlight, Brent had lowered himself to his side, resting on one elbow. His face was turned toward Jake. Almost idly, Brent raised one finger to trace circles around a dark nipple, and the tip of his pink tongue peeked out from between his lips, wetting them.

As horny as he was, Jake suddenly found himself unwilling to use this beautiful man to simply satisfy his body's needs, although that had certainly been his intention when he'd dashed into the tent and fumbled through Brent's bag. Something had changed, had snapped within him like a twig in a twister. For the first time in his life, Jake didn't want to just fuck. He wanted to make love. He wanted to make it last.

Dropping to his knees next to Brent, Jake let the lube and the condom packet fall to the ground. Taking Brent's face between his hands, Jake bent down and kissed him deeply. Lying down, he pressed himself against Brent's body, feeling heat permeate his skin. He wouldn't allow their lips to part for an instant, greedy for Brent's taste. He felt that he couldn't get close enough, even though he'd snaked his arm around Brent's hips and had pulled him even closer until they lay belly to belly.

It was Brent's fervent whisper in his ear, fairly begging Jake to take him that spurred Jake into action. Almost reluctantly, he pulled away from the warmth of Brent's body and allowed Brent to rise to his hands and knees again.

Positioning himself, Jake rubbed his hands over Brent's firm cheeks, loving the way Brent's ass backed into his touch and the way his skin twitched under Jake's palms.

Hissing between his teeth, Jake spread Brent's cheeks, pressing a thumb against the hole that he exposed. Grabbing the lube, Jake squeezed a dollop into the crack of Brent's ass, using his thumb to spread it over Brent's asshole. Slipping a finger in up to his knuckle, Jake gave Brent a teasing taste of what was to come. Another finger slipped in next to the first, but as Brent squeezed them tightly, the heat burning Jake's skin, it was Jake who was given the teaser.

Unable to wait another moment, Jake

quickly sheathed himself in the Trojan and slathered his cock with lube. Rubbing the crown of his erection slowly over Brent's clenching opening, Jake licked his lips as he watched himself breach it, pushing past the tight ring of muscle until the head of his cock disappeared within Brent's body. He paused for a moment, relishing the tightness and the heat, and the way their bodies fit together. Jake's eyes screwed shut and his teeth bared as he slowly pushed himself fully inside.

Jake heard Brent groan at the discomfort caused by Jake's cock pushing into his ass, even with the aid of the lubrication. Angling himself to hit Brent's prostate, Jake smiled as Brent's groans swiftly took on a much more sensual tone, low and soft and needy. Jake was aware when Brent took himself in hand, stroking his cock in rhythm to Jake's slow thrusts, and the thought of Brent's fingers wrapped around the velvet skin of his erection sent a tingle shooting through Jake's balls.

Feeling that Brent was ready, Jake wasted no more time. He began to thrust deeply, his pace quickening until his hips were slapping noisily against the firm flesh of Brent's ass. No matter how badly Jake wanted to draw it out, to make the experience last, he found that he couldn't hold out another moment. Groaning as his climax boiled in his gut, his thrusts grew increasingly hard and erratic until, with a few loud grunts, he lost control and emptied himself, unaware that Brent had already done the same.

His weight pushed them down onto the ground, Jake's body covering Brent's as they both panted for breath. "Damn," he whispered. "Goddamn."

Brent twisted out from under Jake's body. Rolling to his side, he wrapped his arms around Jake's waist. He kissed Jake's neck, nuzzling around for a moment before playfully sucking the tender flesh in between his lips. "Good ride, cowboy," he chuckled.

Jake snorted, then disengaged himself from Brent's arms, sitting up. He removed the condom and chucked it in to the flames. "You wait here; I'll bring us some water to heat up over the fire so we can wash up," he said, waggling a warning finger in Brent's face. "Wrap yourself up in the blanket, and don't go wandering off. We've got rattlers out here." He went over to the pickup, rummaging over the side for a moment before heading over to the river carrying a bucket plucked from the bed of the truck.

Jake placed the bucket of river water near the fire to start warming, then returned to the truck once more. This time he carried back a six-pack of LoneStar, a roll of paper towels, and a brown paper bag.

Using a few paper towels to wipe off the worst of the mess from his hand, Brent tossed them on to the fire and settled in, opening up his blanket to allow Jake to scoot in close to him. Jake produced the paper sack he'd brought and the six-pack of LoneStar beer. The bag contained a few sticks of jerky and a couple of bags of potato chips. Chewing on jerky and swigging beer, the two sat quietly, each lost in thought as they stared at the crackling flames of the fire.

***

It was a companionable silence, easy and comfortable. Brent felt no pressure to make conversation, content to just sit and be. It was a feeling he was not accustomed to, and he wondered about it as he watched sparks float upward over the fire.

Brent's past was speckled with lovers, all of whom had been demanding in one way or another, always wanting something from him. After sex, Brent had always felt obligated to utter declarations of affection that he had never really felt or meant. Jake asked for nothing, but seemed to simply want to sit quietly, happy to share a stick of teeth-cracking jerky and a beer in silence.

What disturbed Brent was not the lack of conversation, but the words of endearment that he suddenly found dancing on his tongue, wanting to be said out loud. There was something about this unpretentious cowboy that intrigued Brent, warmed the pit of his stomach, and made him feel connected to another human being in a way he'd never experienced before.

Amazingly, for the first time *he* was the one wanting to hear comforting words. He was stunned to find that he no longer had any driving ambition to go to Dallas, instead hoping that the car part got lost in transit or that Billy Joe Flynt got lost on his way back from his fishing trip. He simply didn't want to leave. He didn't want to leave this quiet, peaceful riverbank, and he definitely didn't want to leave the arms of the handsome cowboy who sat next to him. This sudden and odd urge to stay put with someone he'd barely met scared the hell out of him. What frightened him even more was the compelling urge he was feeling to tell Jake exactly what he was thinking.

Clamping his mouth shut tight around the stick of dried jerky, Brent forced himself to remain silent; watching as steam slowly began to rise from the water bucket.

Chapter Three

Morning sun found them still asleep inside the pup tent, Brent lying on his side and Jake spooned up against him, one arm thrown over Brent's waist. Jake's eyes cracked open, and he smiled an amused half-smile at Brent's soft snores. Jake had enjoyed himself like never before with Brent. It wasn't just the sex. No, it was more than that. It was a feeling Jake had that Brent had *understood* him, without Jake having to try to put what he was feeling into words.

But he did have to admit to himself that the sex had been incredible. He lifted the blanket a bit, allowing his eyes to roam over Brent's trim body, and his cock began to stir as he remembered how good it had felt to be buried deep inside that ass.

Then he looked at his watch.

"Holy shit!" he yelled, sitting bolt upright, still squinting at the round face of his old-fashioned wind-up. "It's eleven-fucking-o'clock in the goddamn morning!" He elbowed Brent, who sputtered awake.

"Get up, get up! I'm going to be late!" Jake yelled, already thrusting his feet into his jeans.

"What's the rush? Late for what?" Brent mumbled, still heavy with sleep and trying to curl back up into the warmth of Jake's arms.

"For the rodeo! I have to be there before one o'clock or else I'll lose my spot! Get dressed, and hurry!" Jake ordered, throwing Brent's clothes over his sleepy face.

Brent had just finished buttoning his shirt when the pup tent began to collapse in around him. He scuttled out of the small triangular opening and stood hopping on one foot as he pulled a sock on over the other.

He put his shoes on in the truck as Jake sped hell-bent-for-leather over the rough roads, redlining it all the way to the rodeo arena. They pulled into the crowded dirt lot of the Webster Memorial Arena with five minutes to spare.

Brent followed Jake as the cowboy sprinted over to an office trailer near the bull-pens, leaving him outside to babysit Jake's duffle bag. When Jake came back, Brent was leaning back against the trailer. Jake re-emerged with a white sheet of cardboard clutched in his hand that bore the number "seven" written on it in large, black block lettering.

"Number seven to ride," Jake explained, pinning the number to his chest. "Lucky seven. I scored in the top twelve among the riders yesterday, so I qualified to ride in the finals' short-go today." He leaned down, unzipped his duffle bag and pulled out his riding rope, glove, protective vest, and his chaps.

"Congratulations," Brent said, smiling, reaching out and touching the butter-soft leather of Jake's chaps. They were dark brown, fringed, and intricately tooled, with stars of contrasting cream-colored leather decorating them.

"You can congratulate me after I go my eight seconds today and don't get tore up in the process." Jake said, grinning. "I drew Heartache Road this go-round." He put on his chaps, buckling the wide strips of leather at his waist and around his muscular thighs, tucked his riding glove into his back pocket, and donned his protective vest. He slipped his bull rope over his right shoulder, a pair of tin cowbells jangling from one end.

"Let's pretend that I didn't understand a word of what you just said," Brent replied, looking Jake over with an amazed expression. "Because I didn't. What or where is Heartache Road?"

Jake grinned, seeing Brent's concern and understanding the reason behind it. The man didn't want to see Jake get hurt. Fair enough, and it gave Jake a warm feeling in his belly but, Jake thought, that sure as shit wasn't going to stop him from getting on the back of that bull.

"Heartache Road is the name of the bull I'm going to ride this afternoon. I have to stay on him for eight seconds, or I'll get a no-score. To win the money and the buckle, I have to have the highest score... the best ride," he explained as he led Brent closer to the bullpens. "That's him... That's Heartache Road."

Brent's eyes followed Jake's finger, pointing at a brown bull with a white-splattered pattern marking its body. The creature was enormous, closing in on two thousand pounds of muscle and attitude. Snot dripped from its nose and its eyes rolled up white as it banged its side against the steel of the bullpen, rattling it.

***

Brent, who had no experience with animals other than a dog he'd owned when he was a boy, could see that this beast was not one to be taken lightly.

"Holy shit! You're going to *ride* that thing?" Brent asked, feeling the blood drain from his face. "It's got fucking *horns*!" he added, not quite sure why the horns bothered him even more than the sheer size of the bull, except that he had a sudden, gory image of Jake impaled on the bull's head, being shaken and tossed about like a rag doll.

Jake laughed, clapping his hand on Brent's shoulder. "The horns are the least of my worries. The tips are sawed off, although they can still cause a heap of damage. It's his feet that worry me more. Picture getting stepped on by something that weighs as much as your car! Besides, I have no intention of getting bucked-off or stepped on," he said. "That rank bastard owes me a ride. He bucked me off twice a couple of weeks ago." Jake turned his head and spat. "Come on, we're going to start soon, and I want to watch the other riders."

He led Brent to the competitor's stage, a wooden set of bleachers located above and be-hind a pair of steel bucking chutes. They stood and watched as one after another rider burst from the chute, only to be thrown by their bull before the whistle had sounded their eight sec-onds. Only one rider thus far had managed to keep his seat. Jake explained that the score he had to beat was eighty-four.

"I'm up soon. I have to go," Jake whis-pered to Brent. He stared at Brent for a second as though he wanted to kiss him, but moved away at the last moment and trotted down to the area behind the chutes.   Brent watched for a few minutes Jake warmed up, stretching the muscles of his arms and legs. He looked like every cowboy Brent had ever seen on the silver screen. He thought to himself that he'd love to see Jake wearing *nothing* but the hat and the chaps, smiling for a moment at the mental picture he gave himself, before turning his attention back to Jake and the bull.

Jake sidled over to a chute where the white-splattered bull was waiting. With the help of another rider, he set his riding rope around the belly of Heartache Road.

From where he stood, Brent could see Jake climb over and lower himself over the rail, into the chute and on top of the bull's broad back. He watched as Jake finagled with his riding rope that now encircled the bull's powerful chest and seemed to be strapping his right hand down under it. Leaning over the railing of the stage, Brent clenched his fingers around the cool metal until his knuckles whitened, his eyes never leaving Jake.

Suddenly, in a furious flurry of motion, the chute opened and the bull exploded out of it, carrying Jake with him.

His free hand held high in the air, using his arm like a rudder to keep his balance, Jake clung tenaciously to its back as the bull bucked and jumped, desperately trying to rid itself of its rider. The bull's head would lower while its hindquarters kicked and twisted in the air, its entire body spinning first in one direction than the other. The raw power of the bull and the strength of the rider were evident as one fought to rid itself of its burden and the other fought to stay put.

It was the longest eight seconds of Brent's life.

Just when Brent had become certain that time had stopped, the whistle blew and Jake flew off the bull's back, landing hard and bouncing a couple of times in the sawdust of the arena. Two men, their faces painted as clowns, rushed in trying to get the bull's attention away from Jake, who lay sprawled out on the ground of the arena, stunned by the particularly hard dismount.

The bull made short dashes toward one or another of the rodeo clowns and seemed to allow itself to be herded toward the exit into the pen. Without warning, it suddenly spun around and charged back toward Jake, who had just managed to stand up. He hit the fence running and scampered up a heartbeat before the bull plowed into it, the steel fence shuddering under the impact. A cowboy on horseback rode up and lassoed the bull, leading it away.

Brent's scream was frozen in his throat as he watched in horror, certain that Jake was about to be trampled into the sawdust by the charging ton of misery called Heartache Road. His relief at seeing Jake perched, albeit precariously, on the top of the fence as the bull rammed it just below his dangling feet, caused tears to prick at the corners of Brent's eyes. His knees felt weak, his heart was hammering, and he thought for a moment that he was going to either vomit or pass out.

Handed his bull rope and hat by one of the rodeo clowns, Jake's dark blue eyes twinkled and his face split in a broad, cocky grin. Jake lifted his hat in the air and waved it, looking toward Brent and yee-hawing with pride over his successful ride. He hopped over the other side of the chute and made his way back toward the competitor's stage, the recipient of repeated backslapping and handshaking by the admiring crowd.

Brent jumped off the stage and ran around the back of the bleachers, meeting Jake halfway in a fierce hug. He pulled back, looking into Jake's beaming face, not sure if he wanted to kiss him or deck him.

"You scared the fucking shit out of me!" Brent finally yelled, angrily pushing Jake away. He frowned then lunged forward, pulling Jake into a crushing bear hug, knocking the cowboy's hat off. "I thought it was going to kill you!"

Jake patted Brent on the back, chuckling. "You get used to it. I'm fine. Shh...there's my score," he said, pulling away from Brent and picking his hat up from the ground.

"Jake Goodall, 44 and a half. Heartache Road, 45," the announcer's deep voice boomed over the loudspeaker.

"Goddamn!" Jake cried, throwing his Stetson up into the air. "They're going to have to go a long way to beat that!" He laughed, shouldering Brent, then bent down and picked up his hat again, swatting the dust off it before replacing it on his head.

Jake looked around a moment, then grabbed Brent's arm and pulled him into the darkness underneath the stands. His mouth was on Brent's instantly, his hands sliding down, kneading his ass through Brent's chinos.

Jake kissed him hungrily, clearly turned on by the excitement of his ride and Brent couldn't help but respond in kind. Jake smelled of the bull, sawdust, sweat, and leather, and Brent found that the scent was an amazing aphrodisiac. For a moment, both of them forgot that they were standing beneath a set of bleachers full of spectators, any one of whom might glance down at any time and see two men lost in each other's arms and mouths.

Pulling away, Jake rested his chin on Brent's shoulder, breathing harder than he had after his ride.

"I have to be careful here," he whispered, glancing up toward the stands. "It ain't like Dallas or New York, you know."

Brent hugged Jake close for a moment, then pulled away to look at him. "What do you mean?" he asked, his stomach tightening and his brows knitting as he felt the beginnings of anger stir. "This is the twenty-first century and a free country, last time I checked. What the fuck do we care what people think?"

"This ain't New York, Brent. It's not the same. People here don't cotton much to men like us," Jake answered in a hoarse whisper.

"Men like us? What is that supposed to mean?"

"You know what I mean."

"Cowboys and computer software sales-men? I can always tell people that I drive a beer truck, if it'll make them feel better."

"No, you don't, and I'm being serious here, Brent. You know that ain't it. It's just that we don't go broadcasting our own personal business. They just don't understand. They... well, things can happen."

Brent sighed, looking down and to the side for a moment. He knew exactly what Jake meant. He'd felt it himself in the bar, that subtle, uneasy feeling - that uncomfortable sensation of feeling different and knowing that to the people around you, *different* equated to *threatening*. Everybody knew everybody here, and knowing that Jake was with Brent and not just as a friend, could cause the cowboy some serious problems.

"Yeah, I understand. Jake," Brent asked, chewing on his lower lip, "What's happening here? I mean... I just *met* you for God's sake, but I feel... I don't know *what* I feel. Connected, maybe." He risked a glance at Jake, worried that he was putting the cowboy off with his confession. "I do know that all of a sudden I'm not in any hurry to get my car fixed."

Jake smiled, and Brent could see an embarrassed flush on his cheeks. Jake folded his arms across his chest and tucked his chin down to hide his face. "Yeah? You want to know a secret? I never brought anybody up to that place by the river before. It's always been my own spot, where I go to think things through and be by myself. But when I met you I didn't even have to think about where to bring you. I knew. I wanted to be there with you," he said softly, scuffing the dirt with his boot heel. Then his eyes flicked up, a mischievous light in them. "Damn near killed you while I was at it."

Brent laughed. "Well, I'm not dead yet. So, what do we do now?" he asked, taking Jake's Stetson from his head and plopping it on top of his own dark hair.

Grinning, Jake said, "We wait to see if my score holds and I win. Then we can go celebrate." The warmth in his eyes told Brent what the 'celebrating' was going to entail. Jake took his hat back and set it on his head again, then led Brent out from under the bleachers and back up to the competitor's stand.

The last of the cowboys had his go-around, but couldn't beat Jake's score. Jake's name was announced as the winner, and with a whoop and a holler he proudly trotted out to the middle of the arena under the cheers of the crowd to accept his check and a fancy silver belt buckle embossed with a bull and rider on it.

Brent waited patiently for Jake to receive his accolades, leaning against the railing of the competitor's stand and feeling as proud as if he'd won it himself. A deep, grating voice from behind him drew his attention away from the cowboy standing in the middle of the arena.

"Didn't I see you at the Lobo last night?"

Turning, Brent found himself facing a bear of a man, craggy-faced and not looking very friendly at all. "You might have. I was there."

"Yeah you was. And you left with that cowboy, didn't you?" the man asked, pointing his chin toward the center of the arena where Jake still stood with the rodeo officials. "There's been some talk about that boy. Now a city dude comes to town and waltzes out of the bar with him, then shows up at the rodeo with him the next day, acting closer than kissin' cousins. What's that tell a man?"

"That he's a bull rider and that a friend came to see him ride," Brent said in a tight, flat voice. He'd known men like this before, eager to fight and threatened by something they couldn't understand. Until now, he'd been lucky enough to have escaped a close encounter like this with no more than a few insults.

Brent's skin tingled as a finger of fear crawled down his spine and tickled at his scrotum. The man's fists were curled into balls, and he looked as though he might just take a swing at Brent right there in the open. Brent wondered if anyone here might stop him, or if the crowd would just cheer him on like a schoolyard bully beating on the most unpopular kid in class.

"That better be *all* there is to it. We take rodeo seriously in these parts, mister. It wouldn't do to find out we been givin' champion buckles to a faggot," the man growled ominously. "Wouldn't do a'tall to see two growed men pawin' each other right under the spectator stands. It ain't right. It ain't natural. People 'round here ain't goin' to tolerate it in their own backyards. Best if you turn around now and head back to wherever it is you're from, afore somebody gets hurt. You been warned." He turned on his heel and walked away, leaving Brent staring slack-jawed at his back.

Brent shook his head, unable to believe that he'd just been threatened by some John Wayne wannabe in a red-checked flannel shirt. He'd had his share of angry looks and foul name-calling in his day, but he'd never been threatened like that before, and he wasn't sure what to do about it. He was still looking stunned when Jake returned.

"What's wrong? What happened?" Jake asked immediately, seeing the look on Brent's face.

"It's nothing… don't worry about it. Nothing I can't handle," Brent answered, finding a smile for his friend. "Can I congratulate you now? You won!" He grinned. "Let me see your buckle, cowboy!" There was no way he was going to ruin Jake's big moment with the ugly truth.

"Something's wrong."

"*Nothing's* wrong," Brent insisted, turning the shining buckle over in his hands. He handed it back to Jake. "Come on. I'm starving. Let's go get something to eat, okay?"

Nodding slowly, Jake kept silent and walked with Brent back to his pickup truck. He threw his equipment into the truck bed and placed the buckle and the check in the glove compartment.

"I guess we could grab a bite at one of the stands on the fairgrounds, if you don't mind cheap hotdogs or gritty hamburgers. Or, better still, we can go back to my folks' house. Ma will fix us some lunch."

"Your mother?" Brent raised an eyebrow. "Your family knows about you liking other men? They won't mind you bringing me home?"

"Nah, of course they don't know. It'd break my mother's heart and my old man would have a stroke – after he beat the living shit out of me. You're just a friend, that's all," Jake replied, shrugging his shoulders, spots of color appearing high on his cheeks and his mouth set in a grim line. "I want to show them my buckle anyway. Old man's always going off on how the rodeo is a waste of time and how I should give up dreaming but this check should shut him up for a while, at least." Jake sighed heavily, shaking his head. "You don't tell people around here that you don't like girls. It just ain't done, Brent. Nobody would understand."

"Maybe not," Brent said thoughtfully, as

Jake started up the truck and pulled out of the lot, "But hiding who you are is no way to live, Jake. When I first came out I thought my family was going to disown me. It took my parents a while, but they eventually came around to accept it." Brent paused, then chuckled. "Then again, my mother still tries to set me up on dates with her friends' daughters."

"You're a lucky man, Brent Miller. I'd give anything not to have to pretend to be something I ain't."

Brent was silent for a moment as they drove down the highway, feeling a lump form in his throat. "Can you pull over for a minute?" Brent suddenly asked.

Jake frowned, but nodded. "You going to be sick?" he asked.

"No, but there's something else that I need to take care of that's really urgent," Brent replied, smiling sadly. In that one sentence, Jake had let him know how lonely his life had been and it was ripping a hole in Brent's heart.

"Well, then, what in the hell is it that's so all-fire important?" Jake asked, frowning at Brent. "You're acting a mite peculiar." He seemed anxious to get to his folks' house to show off his newly won buckle. "If you have to pee, just aim the damn thing out of the window. I'm hungry."

Brent ignored Jake's question and jerked his thumb toward the side of the road.

Jake pulled over onto the shoulder of the

highway, and as soon as the truck stopped rolling he turned and looked at Brent. "Well? I'm a-waiting. What is it that you have to do?"

Brent scooted over across the seat and fisted his fingers in Jake's shirt, pulling him in close. Lifting one hand, he caressed the bristling shadow that covered the cowboy's cheek, then leaned in and kissed him with all the passion he could muster.

Breaking away, Jake smiled. "Now what's gotten into your britches? Not that I'm complaining, mind you."

"That was for being stronger than I could ever hope to be," Brent answered, the tone of his voice telling Jake that he wasn't talking about physical strength. "For putting up with small-mindedness and meanness and still turning out as fine as you have. You deserve better than this, Jake Goodall."

Jake remained silent, and instead of speaking he gave Brent a curt nod, his mouth clamping shut tightly but his chin trembling a bit. Clearing his throat, he threw the truck in drive again and took to the road.

Brent smiled, sliding back over toward the passenger side door, content that he'd made Jake feel special and wanted. He *was* special, Brent realized, and Brent *did* want him. Now he just needed to work out how to keep him.

Chapter Four

Jake's family home turned out to be an old, slightly tilted two-story farmhouse on about twenty acres of land. As Jake explained, the Goodalls kept a small vegetable garden and a few horses, chickens, and a goat named Blue, but their living was provided by Jake's father's feed store in the town of West Fork, about five miles west.

He led Brent up onto the creaking wrap-around porch, then opened the front door and hollered for his mother. "Ma? Company, Ma!" he called, taking off his hat and leading Brent into the front parlor.

The parlor could have been plucked up from the 1940's and set down right there in the middle of modern day Texas. The sofa and two wing chairs were upholstered in dusty brown velvet, so threadbare in places that the springs were likely to poke through, as lumpy as oatmeal in others, and shiny all over from who knew how many years of rear-ends setting on them. Oval rag-rugs sat on the rough pine plank flooring. A few spindly tables were covered with fragile hand-crocheted doilies in yellow and white yarn, one holding a tarnished

brass lamp with a yellowed, fringed lamp-
shade. A stack of magazines - none of which
looked as though they dated later than the early
nineties - were piled on the coffee table, along
with a bowl of plastic fruit.

The windows were hung with sheer white
curtains, shredded where they met the win-
dowsills from what might have been cat claws.
One of the possible perpetrators, a fat gray
tabby, was sitting on the sill just behind the
curtains, its tail hanging down and swishing
over the sill like a pendulum.

An impressive brick fireplace, its hearth
blackened with decades of use, dominated one
end of the room. Above it was hung a fading
but neatly framed embroidery of The Lord's
Prayer. Sharing the spot of honor above the
mantle with the embroidery was a huge rack of
eight-point deer antlers, mounted with equal
care. A cherry-wood clock and a few odd
pieces of ceramic bric-a-brac were spread out
evenly across the mantle.

Stepping out from the adjacent kitchen,
Jake's mother nodded politely at Brent when
Jake introduced him. She was a thin, grayed
woman with a grim mouth set in a face lined
with a half-century of troubles.

The only time light came into her eyes was
when Jake showed her his buckle. Then the
years seemed to peel away and she was a
young girl again watching her first rodeo, back
when life was full of possibilities. She ran a

dishwater-reddened finger across the shiny silver surface of the buckle, and smiled up into her son's face. Then, just as quickly as the light had come, it receded, leaving her again a woman old before her time in a thin, snap-down housedress and frayed slippers.

"Y'all go show your friend around and get cleaned up, Jake, while I get dinner on," she said, nodding again toward Brent.

She turned to go back into the kitchen, then paused a moment, her hand falling to trace the battered black cover of an old Bible that sat on the arm of the sofa. Her eyes darted from Jake to Brent and back again, an unspoken accusation flickering in them. "Your daddy's out back in the barn." Without another word she disappeared into the kitchen, and the sounds of pots and pans clattering reached Brent's ears.

Jake stared for a moment at the doorway to the kitchen, then turned to Brent and summoned up a smile. "Well, guess we ought to go out back." He led Brent back out the front door and around the side of the house.

"What was *that* all about?" Brent asked as they walked down the sun-bleached steps onto the dirt. He was wondering about the cool look Jake's mother had given them before leaving the parlor.

"My ma is sharper than anyone ever gives her credit for, that's what. She sees you with me, and it gives her ideas," Jake replied. He avoided meeting Brent's eyes, looking away and hooking his thumbs in the pockets of his jeans. "Guess she's thinking I'll be toasting on the devil's campfire someday."

"That's ridiculous," Brent said, then noticed the pained look on Jake's face. Wisely, he decided to change the subject. "Do you live here with your folks, Jake?" Brent asked. He looked up toward the second floor of the house where a pair of yellow curtains fluttered at an open window.

"No, I got a little trailer over on the other side of the property down toward the road. You can see it from here, though," Jake explained, pointing toward the west. Brent squinted a bit and saw the dying sun's rays reflecting red off an aluminum surface in the distance.

They walked toward the barn, a large square and dark red building, trimmed with white and set back from the house. A small, split-rail corral was adjacent to it and a couple of horses, both chestnut in color and slightly swaybacked, stood drinking from a trough within it, long black tails swishing lazily.

Pausing before entering the barn, Jake turned to Brent and said, without quite meeting Brent's eyes, "Don't take offense to anything my Pa might say in there. He's a tough ol' bird, speaks his mind. He doesn't mean anything by it."

Brent nodded and patted Jake on the

shoulder. Following him into the dim, cool recesses of the barn, he spotted a tall, gray-haired man, his shoulders stooped from years of hard work, pitching hay into a stall.

"Pa? This here's Brent Miller, a friend of mine. He's staying for supper."

The tall man turned, leaning on the handle of the pitchfork and frankly appraised Brent. "You with the rodeo, boy?" he asked, in a voice as rough as his looks.

"No, sir."

"Smart fella. I keep trying to get it through my son's head to give up that nonsense before he gets his skull busted open, but he won't listen. Someday they're gonna be scooping his brains up from the sawdust with a shovel. Ain't no reason for it except pure foolishness, if you ask me. No money in it no how either, not in the rinky-dinky rodeos around here."

Brent shook his head at Jake's father. "I'm afraid I don't agree with you. I don't believe that it's foolishness, Mr. Goodall. Jake won first place today. He won a buckle and a check," he said, cutting his eyes toward Jake, who looked back at him as if a strong breeze might blow him over. "It was the best ride I'd ever seen," Brent continued, fudging the truth a bit. Jake's ride had been the only ride he'd ever seen, but Jake's father didn't need to know that.

Defending Jake might not win any points for Brent with Jake's father, but at the moment

Brent didn't care in the slightest. He'd seen how the man's words had affected his son. Seeing the dumbstruck look on Jake's face when Brent had defended him had given Brent a sudden inspiration and the words fell out of his mouth as naturally as breathing. "As a matter of fact, I'm going to sponsor Jake on the pro circuit." He kept his focus trained on the elder Goodall, although Brent could feel Jake's eyes boring holes through his skin.

"That a fact?" Ray Goodall said, his bushy white eyebrows lifting in surprise. "You're going to give my boy money to ride? Why?" he asked, his eyes narrowing suspiciously.

"As an investment, Mr. Goodall. I'm a businessman, sir. I've seen Jake ride and I believe that he can be a champion. I'll front him the money, and take a percentage of the winnings. The rest of the prize money goes to Jake," Brent explained, hoping that what he was saying would make sense, considering he was making it up as he went along.

"Well, then… I suppose that's all right, if you want to throw your money away like that. You married, Mr. Miller?"

 Jake's father asked, throwing a curve from left field at Brent.

Brent, however, made his living among the cutthroats and sharks in an industry that was notorious for feeding frenzies, and in a city that would chew you up and spit you out if you couldn't think on your feet.

"No, sir. Still looking. Haven't found a girl yet that I wanted to marry," he answered smoothly. Not the truth, but not exactly a lie, either.

The older man grunted and turned back to his work, muttering something under his breath that sounded suspiciously like "ain't looking too hard either, I bet."

After watching his father pitch hay for a few moments, Jake looked down at the buckle in his hand. Slipping it into his back pocket, he turned to Brent. "We ought to go wash up before dinner."

Giving Jake's father a last look that would have told the old man exactly what Brent thought of him had he turned around in time to see it, Brent walked out of the barn following Jake, who led him out to the far side of the corral where they couldn't be overheard.

"What in the hell was that about?" Jake hissed, putting one foot up on the bottom rail of the fence and folding his arms over his chest. He glared at Brent, waiting for an answer.

"Just what I said. I'll sponsor you, if you want me to," Brent answered. "I know I should have asked you first, but he was really pissing me off in there."

"He's always like that. I told you before that it doesn't mean anything."

"It means plenty. I saw your face, Jake. You can't tell me that it doesn't hurt that he doesn't believe in you," Brent said, his tone softening at the pain that flashed in Jake's eyes. "I meant what I said, Jake. I'll sponsor you. I've got the money, and you've got the talent."

"That the only reason you're doing it? The money?" Jake asked, looking out at the horses. "Because there ain't no guarantee that I'll even make it far enough to qualify for the finals and the big cash."

There was a pause as Brent carefully considered his words. "I'd be lying if I said it was," he finally answered. "The truth is that I've been trying all day to think of a way to… well, to not have to say goodbye. That's crazy, isn't it? Shit, I sound like a stalker. We only met yesterday, but I can't seem to help myself. I want to get to know you better, Jake. I want you to get to know me, too. If that's what you want. Whether you decide to let me sponsor you is your decision, though. I swear that whether or not you decide that you'd like to see me won't have anything to do with it."

When Jake looked back toward Brent his eyes were misty and he quickly tipped his head down, letting the brim of his hat hide his eyes. "I can't promise you that I'd win," he said. "Can't promise you anything, really."

"I don't expect you to. You don't know me any better than I know you. But last night… that *meant* something, you know? If you had asked me before we left the bar what I thought was going to happen, I'd have told you that I was just going to get laid. But as it turned out, it wasn't just a quick and easy fuck, Jake. Not to me. It was wonderful – you were wonderful - but afterwards, just sitting and being with you was even better."

Jake nodded his head. "So what happens now?" he asked, studying the wood grain of the fence and picking at it with his fingernails. "Where's that put us?"

"If you want me to sponsor you, then I guess you can say that we're business partners. I'll front you the money and take twenty percent of the take. As far as you and me… I suppose that we just take it one step at a time."

"Fair enough," Jake replied, nodding his head again. "I want to think about it, though. Going pro is a big decision. I'd have to quit my job at Pa's feed store for one thing, so I'd be free to travel to events…" He took off his hat, raked his fingers through his tousled hair and changed the subject. "We ought to go wash up before dinner. Ma'll have my hide if I stink up the table. C'mon, we can pretty-up at the trailer," he added, leading Brent toward his pickup.

Jake's trailer was not much more than an oversized, dented aluminum can set on wheels. An ancient Airstream, it contained a tiny kitchenette with a knee-high refrigerator and a two-burner propane stove, a closet-sized bathroom, and a double bed set at the back. Brent could see Jake's mother's hand at work in the hand-stitched quilt that covered the bed and in the faded gingham curtains that hung crookedly over the two small windows. Outside, a generator hummed and whined.

Brent sat on Jake's bed in nothing but his skin, his toiletry bag set on the floor at the foot of the bed, listening to the splattering sound of the shower. So small that one man could barely fit inside the plastic stall, Jake had waited until Brent had finished showering before taking his own, much to Brent's disappointment. He would have liked to have the opportunity to slide a bar of soap over the hard muscles of Jake's body, and then maybe have a turn at sliding something else *somewhere* else.

The water dribbled to a stop and Jake stepped out of the bathroom, wrapping a towel around his waist. He eyed Brent, cocking an eyebrow at the evidence of Brent's soapy fantasy. "Now, what in tarnation could you have *possibly* been thinking about?" he asked sarcastically, his cheek lifting with a knowing smirk.

Brent shrugged sheepishly, figuring that the answer was obvious.

"Got yourself a little problem there, huh?" Jake teased, folding his arms across his bare chest, staring pointedly at Brent's erection.

"Little?" Brent answered, quirking his own brow at Jake.

"Small?"

"*Small*?"

"Gonna call you 'Tiny' from now on," Jake grinned, laughing outright at the exaggeratedly shocked expression on Brent's face.

Brent jumped up from the bed, grabbing Jake around his shoulders and pushing him down onto the mattress, growling in mock anger. He ripped the towel open and straddled Jake, pleased to see that he was developing a hard-on of his own. "Does this look *small* to you, cowboy?" he asked, rubbing his cock along the length of Jake's.

"Well, now that I see it up close and all it don't look *that* small…"

"Damn straight," Brent smiled, closing his eyes and rocking his hips, enjoying the sensation of their cocks rubbing against one another.

"…*Tiny*," Jake finished, chuckling.

With an affronted gasp, Brent paused, smirking down at Jake with narrowed eyes. "Full of salt today, aren't you?" He playfully flicked one of Jake's rosy nipples, eliciting a hissed oath. Bending over to the side of the bed, Brent reached down into his bag, fumbling blindly through the contents. Removing the tube of lube and a condom, he squeezed a puddle of gel into the palm of his hand before tossing the tube back into his bag.

"Now, what exactly do you plan on doing with *that*?" Jake asked. His stomach muscles clenched under Brent's thighs, as if he was ready to buck Brent off him. "It ain't gonna be that way, Brent."

"What way is that?" Brent asked, taking both of their cocks in his greased hand and sliding his fist over them, stroking them in tandem.

"I ain't the cow, and you ain't the bull," Jake murmured, placing his hands on Brent's hips, relenting and tilting his pelvis up into Brent's hand. "Cowboys don't get ridden. It's them that does the riding."

"That so? Is the big, strong wrangler afraid of this *little* thing?"

There was a pregnant pause, and Brent could feel every muscle in Jake's body tense.

"I'm not playing, Brent."

The stern note in Jake's voice brought Brent up short and gave him reason to wonder. "You're serious? You expect to top *all* of the time?" he asked, his fist holding both of their cocks immobile. "Jake, I don't mind you fucking me – as a matter of fact, I enjoyed it a lot – but every now and then I'd like to be the one drilling for oil, Texan."

"Then we've got ourselves a problem, don't we?" Jake replied as his mouth set itself in a stubborn line.

Brent found himself at a loss for words. He hadn't considered the possibility that Jake might be one of those men who were emphatic and uncompromising about their chosen role, and he had to wonder to himself if he were willing to remain the passive partner should their relationship continue.

He realized that in this case it was not only a matter of preference but of trust and respect, neither of which he'd had the time to foster with Jake in this, the fragile beginning of their affair. Jake had spent his entire life in hiding, listening to degrading and Philistine humor, subject to the homophobic views held by nearly everyone he knew. Brent was almost certain that in Jake's mind, to allow a man to fuck him would be tantamount to losing what little masculinity he thought he possessed. It was going to take a lot of time and a load of patience to help Jake get past that, and Brent questioned whether or not he was up to the task.

Perhaps it might be best to end it now, to stand up, get dressed, and walk away before Brent invested emotionally in a man whose point of view might never mesh with Brent's own. Chalk it up to a pleasant interlude that had livened up an otherwise unplanned and unfortunate visit to a flyspeck town in the middle of nowhere. An anecdote to be shared over margaritas with Brent's more enlightened friends in New York.

Brent was close to doing just that, close to telling Jake that he was right, that they did have a problem. He was ready to agree that he and Jake had come to an impasse and that it might be best to simply call it a day and go their separate ways. But Brent's resolve faltered as he remembered the way Jake had looked at him the night before.

No one had ever looked at Brent that way, as if Brent were a priceless treasure laid out on a velvet cloth rather than just a gay man from New York lying in the dirt next to a small campfire. Jake had treated him as if Brent were the Holy Grail with worth beyond measure. It had been a heady feeling and one that Brent admitted he was loath to give up easily. Brent realized that if he walked away now, he might never again find anyone who made him feel that way.

Looking down at Jake, whose cheeks had colored and who was beginning to move as if to slide out from under Brent, he came to a decision.

Nodding almost to himself and tenderly pushing a hank of wet hair out of Jake's eyes, Brent smiled, placing the still-wrapped condom to the side.

"No, we don't, Jake. It's fine."

***

Jake didn't answer, but continued to eye Brent suspiciously. That the man had assumed that Jake would lie still and spread his legs for him was a blow to Jake's ego, and he watched Brent carefully, trying to discern whether he was speaking the truth.

Shades of gray didn't exist in Jake's life. Everything was black or white, up or down, right or wrong. Between them lay a fine line, razor sharp and unwavering, and Jake had managed to carefully walk that line for nearly all of his life. His balance was precarious. One misstep and he'd tumble off, his secret exposed.

But Brent was like a fierce wind blowing across the prairie, threatening to sweep Jake off his feet and send him flying headfirst from his unstable position. He'd kept himself on a safe, short leash for a long time, but because of Brent Jake was very close to admitting to himself that he wanted to be set free, wished for it, *ached* for it. Freedom never came without cost. In Jake's case, the cost was exposure and he feared it was too steep a price for him to pay. If Jake allowed Brent to dominate him, it would be tantamount to throwing his arms open wide and admitting to the world at the top of his voice which side of the fence he really walked, and that scared Jake shitless.

Digging in his heels, Jake steeled himself, stubbornly determined to hold onto his place on the line.

***

Knowing that he'd unintentionally put a dent in the trust they'd begun to build with each other, Brent did the only thing that he thought would put Jake's mind at ease. He let go of his own cock and took hold of Jake's alone.

Jake's skepticism loomed between them like an invisible wall. Jake's anger had softened his penis, but that was not a deterrent to Brent. Wet sounds filled the silence as Brent's fingers slid along Jake's slicked cock and teased at its delicate foreskin. Still straddling Jake's thighs, Brent braced himself up on one arm, lowering his head until he was able to capture one of Jake's nipples between his teeth. He nipped at the hardening bud until Jake groaned, threaded his fingers into Brent's hair, and began to rock his hips into Brent's fist.

Under Brent's skillful fingers, Jake's cock stiffened until it was as hard and ready as it had been before their little argument. Brent moaned softly as he eyed the hot, turgid flesh he held in his hand, knowing exactly how he would feel when Jake's penis entered him – breached, stretched to his limit, and ultimately completely filled. Brent's asshole clenched repeatedly, as if beckoning to Jake's engorged cock, urging it to hurry. He sat up, unable to wait a moment longer.

Breathing as heavily as Jake, Brent fumbled with one hand over the sheets of the bed for the condom that he had discarded earlier. He gave Jake no time to question his motives as Brent quickly opened the condom and rolled the thin latex down over Jake's erection.

Sheathed in the condom, Brent felt Jake's relief as the tension between them evaporated. Lifting himself up and hissing through his teeth, Brent slowly and carefully lowered himself over Jake's length and impaled himself on it.

***

As hard as Jake tried, he couldn't prevent his body's reaction to the workings of Brent's warm hand and mouth. Brent's hand warmed the lube that covered Jake's cock, squeezing and releasing it in long strokes, reminding Jake of what it had felt like to pound himself deeply into Brent's ass the night before. As he bucked upward into Brent's fist, Jake found himself losing control. He wanted Brent again, now, this instant, and was on the verge of flipping Brent over and asserting his dominance when Brent had suddenly positioned himself over Jake's cock and had done it for him.

As he felt himself guided into Brent's tight ass, the fiery silken walls squeezed every doubt Jake had had out of his mind. Firmly in control again, Jake took over immediately, his hands gripping Brent's hips and holding his weight up; his own hips thrusting his cock upward into Brent's ass even as Brent pushed himself downward.

A thought suddenly burst into Jake's mind

as Brent's ass slapped down hard against
Jake's hipbones making Brent cry out softly.
Brent had selflessly sacrificed something important for Jake, the very thing Jake had been
unwilling to give. Feeling as if he'd been
doused with ice water, Jake realized with a
stab of guilt which of them was the bigger
man. Looking down between them, he watched
Brent begin to stroke himself, not even asking
that much of Jake. Touched deeply by his
epiphany, Jake felt a great wave of tenderness
for Brent sweep through him, and a compelling
need to give something back, however little it
might be.

***

Brent's balls, swelling with lust, bounced
against Jake's dark brown pubic hair as he
took his own cock in hand again, as he had the
night before. It came as a surprise when Jake
batted his hand away and long, work-
roughened fingers closed around Brent's erection.
Looking at Jake, Brent saw that the suspicion
and doubt he'd seen there moments ago had
been replaced by a glistening expression of
affection. In Jake's eyes Brent saw Jake's ap-
preciation of what Brent was willing to give up
for him, and that affected Brent much more
intimately than their physical union. Brent's
spine stiffened and his head snapped back as a

powerful orgasm, roiling up unexpectedly and uncontrollably, overwhelmed him.

His orgasm had barely begun to wane when Brent felt Jake pull free from Brent's body, and Brent silently bemoaned the separation. He would have liked their bodies to remain connected and wished, no matter how irrationally, that there were no latex barrier between them. Brent wanted to feel the hot molten rush fill him as Jake came. Instead, Brent, still trembling with the aftershocks of his own orgasm, contented himself with watching Jake rip the condom off and add his semen to the slick of Brent's that already coated his belly.

Brent leaned down and rested his forehead against Jake's, breathing heavily. "I'll make you a deal, cowboy. I'll never ask you to do anything that you don't want to do, if you'll swear to me the same. It doesn't matter to me if you need to top, Jake. I'll be content as long as I'm with you."

Jake nodded silently in agreement, feeling too sated from his orgasm to speak. He pulled Brent down onto his chest and tucked his chin on top of his head. It felt right to Jake, Brent lying on top of him with only a slick barrier of semen between them, and he was not anxious to get moving.

***

Brent had said that it didn't matter, but

Jake was still not convinced. He refused to allow Brent to get up, holding him firmly with both arms around Brent's back, fearful that when he let go, Brent would get dressed and walk out of the trailer, and out of Jake's life.

After a few moments of cuddling close together, Jake sighed deeply and turned Brent loose, reminding him that his parents would be waiting on them for supper.

Cleaning each other off with the still-damp towel, they quickly dressed. Jake threw on a worn, faded black shirt and lent Brent a clean one, a brown-checked snap-down that was immaculately starched and pressed, to replace the one he'd been wearing since the day before.

Once outside of the trailer, Jake put his hand on Brent's arm and looked at him soberly. "You know where we stand with this, now. If you want to call it quits, I understand."

Brent just smiled, and took Jake's face between his hands. "You listen to me, Jake. It doesn't matter. I don't want to quit anything. Do you?"

With a small smile and a shake of his head, Jake gathered Brent into his arms and kissed him deeply, savoring the softness and warmth of Brent's tongue and the hardness of his body against his own before breaking away. He opened the truck door for Brent before trotting over to the driver's side.

The pickup's engine sputtered to a steady

growl and they headed back over the field to Jake's folks' house for supper.

Neither Jake nor Brent had taken notice of a black Suburban out on the road that had slowed as it passed the trailer before picking up speed and heading down toward a neighboring ranch.

The supper table was covered with a red-checked tablecloth and a blanket of silence. Mrs. Goodall fussed over the fixings, but spent the majority of the meal with her head bent down low over her plate, shuffling food around and managing to get very little into her mouth. Ray Goodall spoke mostly to his wife, and of things of little consequence – how the price of feed was going up, and to make sure she had enough preserves put up to send some over to the Wilsons, who'd had a busted crop from the hailstorms that summer. Neither spoke much to Jake and neither spoke to Brent at all, aside from asking him to please pass the sugar peas.

Dessert came as a relief, since it signaled the end of the torturously uncomfortable supper. They both bid Jake's parents a good night, with Brent thanking them both politely for their hospitality. He might as well have been thanking the cat for all of the response he got from Jake's folks. Both Jake and Brent breathed a deep, grateful sigh when the screen door of the house slammed shut behind them.

Chapter Five

It was late when Jake's pickup pulled into the yellow-striped parking space in front of the door to Brent's motel room. Brent put his hand on the handle of the truck door, then paused and looked back at Jake. They'd already said their goodnights in the shadows of a broken-down, deserted barn that stood like a skeletal sentry a half-mile from the town limits.

"You think about what I said, Jake Goodall. I've got more than enough room for you. We can fly you out to wherever it is you need to be for the rodeos."

"I told you that I'd think about it, Brent, but it still sounds like charity to me."

"It's not charity. We have a partnership, remember? I sponsor you, and you ride. That's the deal. Besides, I told you that I'm not being charitable. I'm being selfish. I want you with me, Jake, and that's the God's honest truth. Promise me that you'll think about it."

Jake nodded, wanting more than anything to follow Brent into his motel room and spend the night but forcing himself to go home instead, knowing that his pickup parked in the motel lot all night would be asking for trouble.

He watched until Brent closed the door before pulling away into the night.

***

The Lobo was nearly deserted at that late hour. With Monday morning and its best friend, the alarm clock, rearing their ugly heads, most folks had headed home long ago. The workday started early on a ranch, usually just as the sun came up. Only three men remained sitting at the Formica-topped bar. The first, a big and burly older man with a face that seemed permanently soured, sat nursing a mug of draft and periodically pounding on the cracked Formica of the bar. The second two, much younger but striking replicas of the first, nodded and grunted periodically in agreement as they lifted shot glasses and downed fiery amber liquor like water.

"Are you sure of what you and Billy saw, Cody?" the older man asked again, his bushy brows knit in a frown that creased his forehead with deep furrows.

One of the two younger men nodded. "Yep. Sure as I'm sitting here, Pa," he answered, his upper lip curling as if he'd just tasted something oily and rancid. "Right down there by the road next to the Goodall place and out in the wide open, if you believe it."

"Makes me sick to my stomach," the second younger man quickly added, knocking

back another shot. All three of them were into
their cups, but he was well on his way to getting very, *very* drunk. Not simply because of
what he and his brother had seen Jake Goodall
doing with that New York man, but because it
reminded him of a dream he'd had just the
night before last while on a fishing trip with
his brother over at the Neches. A dream that
he'd die before revealing; one that had fea-
tured none other than Jake Goodall and had
left his shorts a sticky mess in the morning.

Billy Joe Flynt didn't know how or why
he'd had that dream, but he *did* know that
somehow, someway, it was all Jake's fault.

"That's it, then. They took it too far this
time. First them hugging and whatnot under
the stands at the rodeo and now right out in
plain sight? What's next? Fornicating on the
front steps of the Victory Baptist Church?" Joe
Flynt spat, his face a picture of disgust. "I
warned that sumbitch to get his fairy ass back
to New York. You do it, Billy. Tonight. Right
now. You and your brother teach that pervert
bastard that the God-fearing folk of Stillwater
ain't gonna sit by and let him turn our good ol'
boys into faggots. Don't you touch Jake Goodall; his daddy's a friend. I'll have a talk with
Ray Goodall about straightening out his boy.
But if you let that ass jockey from New York
walk out of here on his own two legs, I'll have
your guts for garters, the two of you!" he ordered, narrowing his bloodshot piggy eyes at

his sons.

They nodded, tossed back a last shot, then made their way outside to Billy's Suburban.

***

Brent threw his toiletry bag down on the bed and faced the empty motel room. He sat on the edge of the bed and fiddled with the television set, desperate for some kind of noise to fill the silence of the room. He found one station that was playing a movie from the sixties, *The Good, The Bad, and The Ugly*. The picture was fuzzy and flickering and threatening to go out all together, but it was better than the alternative. He left it on, since it was the only station that gave him anything but static and snow.

His car would be ready sometime tomorrow - providing that the part had arrived and that the mechanic was back in town - and he needed to get to Dallas in order to secure the new account. If it were up to Brent, he'd just as soon stay put. He hadn't been able to convince Jake to pack up and follow him back to New York even though he'd sworn that he'd relocate them back to Dallas within six months. Although he'd said he would consider it, Brent wasn't at all certain that Jake would agree in the end.

The truth was that Brent missed Jake already. He missed his cocky half-grin, and the playful nature that simmered just below his stern exterior. He missed his twinkling blue eyes and his gravelly drawl, but most of all Brent missed his strong, calloused hands and warm, soft lips, and the way his naked body had felt spooned around Brent's own the night before in the pup tent. When he thought about the possibility of Jake deciding not to take him up on his offer and that Brent might have to drive off without him, his stomach dropped and his eyes burned.

Sighing, Brent stripped off his clothes, setting the borrowed shirt aside. He'd wash it tonight and return it to Jake tomorrow before leaving for Dallas. Hopefully, he'd be making the trip with Jake riding shotgun in his BMW.

The motel shower was just as stingy with its water as it had been when Brent first arrived. Toweling off with a motel towel that felt more like sandpaper than cloth, Brent threw on a pair of cargo pants. Bare-chested and bare-footed, he picked up Jake's shirt, grabbed his room key and some change, and went off in search of the motel laundry.

He found an old washing machine set aside for the motel guests' use in an alcove at the farthest end of the building. Sitting in a puddle of sudsy water, the machine was a Sears Roebuck model and looked as though it might have been older than Brent. Still, it worked, and he bought a small box of detergent from the vending machine. Throwing in the shirt and the suds, he plopped four quarters into the change slot. The machine had two settings, hot and cold, although Brent had his doubts that the "hot" water setting would actually be any different than the "cold" water setting. He set it for "cold" anyway and pressed the start button.

Rumbling and grinding loudly, and shaking so badly that Brent feared for a moment that the machine might actually walk out of the alcove and into the parking lot, the tub filled with water and the agitator began to chug. As soon as the water turned foamy with detergent, Brent closed the lid.

Turning to head back to his room, Brent was startled by a hard, excruciatingly painful knock to the back of his head. Even as his hands flew up to his skull and he wondered what the hell had just happened, his knees gave way. He was out cold before he hit the cement floor.

The first couple of things that Brent became aware of as he regained consciousness was that his skull felt as if it were being split in two, and that he was so overcome by nausea that he felt as though he were going to vomit.

As his wits returned, he realized that he was lying flat on his back in the dirt and that his arms were tied up over his head. He could feel the coarse rope abrading his wrists as he tried to move his hands. The rope led up to a horse, and was tied under the pommel of the saddle. He tried to open his mouth in protest, but realized that he'd been gagged as well as restrained. He kicked his feet and twisted his body, pulling hard against the ropes, trying to get free, but his efforts were ineffective, as much because of the pain in his head and his nausea as they were because of the secure knots in the ropes that held him firm.

His vision was blurry, but he could make out two shadowed shapes in cowboy hats standing over him, looking down at him. A boot shot out and kicked him hard in the ribs. With a sickening crunch, pain shot through his side and made him scream against the rag that had been stuffed into his mouth.

"If it were up to me," one of the men standing over Brent said, "I'd cut your dick off and feed it to you, you cocksucking bastard, but I don't want to have to touch it. Probably diseased and God-all knows what else. Instead, we're gonna teach you how cowboys deal with faggots from New York City like you." The man turned to the other and said, "Mount up and drag him up to the crossroad. That ought to mess this pretty boy up enough so his own mama won't recognize him."

"Ain't we done enough already?" asked the second man in a hoarse whisper. "We already done split his head open, and I'm willing to book that you just took out a couple of ribs. I ain't going to walk the green mile over a faggot, Billy. No way, not even for you and Pa. If we kill him, then the newspapers and television reporters won't let it go 'till they have our asses in a sling and a needle in our arms. You seen what happened with those boys over in Houston… they're like a dog with a bone over stuff like this."

"Just shut up and do it! It's a dirt road, for Christ's sake…it won't kill him. Leastways, I don't think so. And if it does, then there'll just be one less pervert in the world taking up oxygen. He got no right doing what he's been doing with Jake Goodall, Cody. No right."

Brent was fading in and out of consciousness by this point, the pain in his skull rivaled only by the pain in his side. But the first few feet of hard ground scraping at his bare flesh brought him screaming back from the pain-killing darkness.

The horse galloped along the road, its hooves kicking back a cloud of dust as it dragged Brent over the dirt road, bouncing and twisting him as though he were nothing more than a rag doll, the rocks and earth both taking their toll on his hide.

***

Six a.m. saw Jake, red-eyed and weary, pulling into his usual parking spot alongside of the building that housed Goodall's Feed and Supplies. He hadn't slept at all the night before, too torn by Brent's offer to get any rest.

God knew he had wanted to accept. He had wanted to accept the offer right there on the spot and kiss Brent's feet for making it in the first place, but his conscience wouldn't let him do it. He needed to decide and very quickly, but the decision had to be made because he wanted to be with Brent and not simply because he wanted to get out of West Fork and ride the pro circuit. He'd spent the entire night searching his soul for the answer, praying for guidance, and missing Brent badly.

It was funny how someone could grow on you so quickly. Brent wasn't at all how Jake had thought a man from New York would be; he wasn't snobby, and he didn't look down his nose at Jake because he worked in a feed store to pay his bills. The warmth in his brown eyes and his smile had been genuine when Brent told him that he believed in Jake's talent as a rider. He'd also seemed truthful when he told Jake that he wanted to be with him. More than Brent's offer to sponsor him on the professional circuit, Jake truly wanted to believe Brent's profession that he simply wanted to be with him.

Making his decision just as the first pale light had streaked the sky to the east – and once made, Jake wondered how he ever could have debated it in the first place – he felt as if a weight had been lifted from his shoulders.

Jake Goodall was going to New York.

Hurrying, he had thrown every clean article of clothing he could scrounge up into his old, frayed gray duffle bag, along with a comb, a toothbrush, and a half-used stick of Right Guard deodorant. Already holding all of Jake's riding equipment, the material had strained when Jake zipped it shut.

He had driven over to his parent's house, walked in, and turned down an offer for breakfast. He'd thrown his arms around his mother, holding her close and telling her that he loved her. His father had nodded sagely at him, knowing without the frills of hugs and words how Jake felt, and what his boy was planning to do. He wasn't happy, but he wouldn't ruin Jake's opportunity to ride in the pros. As far as Ray Goodall was concerned, that was the only reason his son would be leaving with that city man, and that was as much as anyone had to know. Jake caught a last glimpse of his mother in his rearview mirror, standing on the porch, wringing her hands in her apron as her youngest son sped away down the road.

Knowing that his pay from the week before was at the store, Jake had planned on stopping by before driving over to the motel, banging on Brent's door until the man woke up, and then taking him up on his offer. Jake grinned to himself as he thought about what they would probably to do celebrate. His crotch bulged just thinking about Brent's firm ass and the way Jake was going to ride him on that lumpy hotel mattress. That he and Brent would soon be in New York and able to be with each other whenever they pleased without hiding and wondering who was watching them seemed too good to be true.

He trotted around to the front of the store, picking the store key out from the cluster of metal on his key ring, and was halfway up the walk before he noticed something large and bulky lying across the doorway.

Sprinting the rest of the way, Jake fell to his knees next to the figure lying prone and still across the threshold of the store's doorway. Shock, anger, and fear combined to form the anguished cry that ripped from his throat, echoing in the early morning silence as he looked down at Brent, lying battered and bloody on the stoop.

He'd thought they'd been careful, but they hadn't been careful enough.

***

Soft, intermittent beeping sounds reached his ears as Jake stood just outside of the hospital room door. He knew what they were. They were the sounds of the machines that the doctors had hooked up to Brent, the ones that monitored his vital signs. They should be comforting sounds, Jake's rational mind told him. As long as they kept beeping and buzzing and whooshing it meant that Brent was still alive, but instead they somehow sounded ominous and threatening. He was dreading this, dreading seeing what had been done to Brent. That his new friend and lover was alive at all seemed no less than a miracle to Jake – Brent been beaten and dragged, and Jake was far too familiar with horses not to understand how easily being dragged behind one could have killed Brent.

When he'd first found him lying in front of the store, Jake's panic and subsequent adrenaline rush had kept him from fully appreciating the damage, but now Brent was lying just beyond the door in the Intensive Care Unit of the Sisters of Mercy Hospital, and Jake had had time to calm down. He would be seeing Brent for the first time since rushing him to the hospital emergency room, redlining his pickup all the way to Nacogdoches. At that point, he hadn't given a flying fuck *who* knew how he felt about Brent or whether or not they were more than just friends. The only thought that kept rattling around in Jake's brain was that he was perilously close to losing him.

The ride into Nacogdoches had seemed to take forever.

Besides being nearly overcome with fear and sorrow, Jake was tormented by guilt. He felt himself as much to blame for Brent's condition as whoever the bastards were who had beaten him bloody, dragged him over a rough road and then left him for dead in front of Jake's father's feed store in an obvious message to Jake.

If he hadn't been so goddamn reckless, hadn't gone to the Lobo that night, hadn't struck up a conversation with a beautiful, dark-haired stranger with the selfish hope of getting laid, then Brent would not be clinging to life in a hospital in Nacogdoches, wired up to a dozen different machines. If Jake hadn't invited him to watch him ride, hadn't taken him camping, hadn't brought him to his trailer, then Brent might at this moment be on his way to Dallas, none the worse for wear from his unplanned stopover in Stillwater.

He hadn't left the hospital waiting room for a single moment while Brent was in surgery, spending nearly all of the eight plus hours alternating between pacing the corridors and stopping in the hospital's tiny chapel, his face covered by his Stetson, silently begging, pleading and bargaining with his Maker to let Brent live. It was only after the nurse had come in and told him that Brent had survived the operation that Jake had left to make two phone calls.

He called his own father first. The grief in his son's voice had shocked the elder Goodall and made him realize that the rumors about his son were true after all. The sudden stony silence on the other end of the line told Jake that his secret was out.

Surprisingly, Jake found that he really didn't care.

The sheriff had brought Brent's personal belongings over from the motel, including his cell phone. Pressing the button and calling Brent's parents had been one of the hardest things Jake had ever had to do in his entire life.

The stunned disbelief in Brent's father's voice had been palpable as Jake had introduced himself and, in a tightly controlled voice, had told the man that his son had been seriously injured. Jake had stopped just short of confessing that all of it had been his fault.

The elder Mr. Miller had told Jake that he and Brent's mother would be on the first available flight out of New York, and had thanked Jake for standing by his son. In a halting voice that suddenly sounded very old he had asked Jake, *begged* Jake to tell him that Brent was going to be all right. Jake had had to tell him that Brent was on the fence and that the doctors weren't certain if he would make it. Hanging up the phone, Jake had run out to his pickup and cried like a baby for an hour.

Now, all Jake had left to do was to see Brent.

Chapter Six

Jake took his hat off, running the brim nervously through his fingers, already feeling a lump forming in his throat. Taking a deep breath, he pushed open the door and stepped into the room, the beeps and whooshes of the machinery suddenly growing louder as he walked toward the single bed that sat in the center of the small room.

Brent lay on his back, covered to the chest by a thin, white sheet. He looked impossibly small, as if the damage done to him had shaved inches off his height and pounds off his weight. Brent's eyes were swollen closed, his thick black lashes lying softly against cheeks that were scraped raw in some places and bruised a dark purplish black in others.

His skull had been cracked open like a walnut, and the doctors had had to go in to repair the damage. The right side of his head had been shaved of his blue-black hair during surgery, but was covered now by a thick white bandage. Jake had been told that should Brent survive there was a chance he might not awaken as the same Brent that Jake knew.

Jake was aware that the rest of Brent's body was covered in scratches, scrapes, and cuts, some deep enough to show bone, and ugly bruises. His left arm had been cast in plaster, as had his right leg. A web of plastic tubing led from his right arm to several liquid-filled pouches hanging on an IV pole. Brent's mouth and nose were covered by a plastic oxygen mask that misted with his breath. Running up from under the sheet was an assortment of colored wires that plugged into several different machines.

The doctors had told Jake that Brent had two broken ribs as well, and that one had punctured a lung. That he was breathing on his own was a miracle in and of itself. In addition, Brent's spine had been twisted like a pretzel during the dragging.

Jake sank into a chair placed at Brent's bedside, his hat in his hand. His chin trembled and his chest hitched as he sat silently staring at the battered face of the man who had been a stranger just a couple of days ago, and yet now meant more to Jake than any man he'd ever met.

Within Jake, two emotions raged against one another. The first was the fear that froze his blood, and the second was the fury that boiled it. Wild horses would not be able to drag Jake from Brent's bedside until Brent was past the danger of losing his life – Jake refused to consider the alternative – but at that point the whole of the state of Texas had better sit up and take notice. Because when he found the ones responsible for doing this to Brent, Jake had every intention of killing them and doing so in the slowest, most painful way possible.

If the law failed to do it, then frontier justice would see him avenged. Jake swore it in a soft oath at Brent's bedside, his cheeks streaked with tears.

Nothing marked the passage of time except for the softly beeping machinery and the slowly moving hands of the wall clock. Nurses came and went, adjusting or replacing the IV pouches, checking Brent's bandages and vital signs, and offering a compassionate smile to the cowboy who sat stoically at his bedside, hat in hand.

Night brightened into morning, morning warmed into afternoon, afternoon faded into dusk, the dusk darkened into night and still Jake kept watch. It was near midnight of the second day when a soft moan instantly woke Jake from a light doze. His head jerked up, and he looked into two swollen, dark brown, pain-filled eyes.

"Hey," Jake said softly, leaning forward and lightly touching one finger to the back of Brent's hand. "'Bout time you woke up, you lazy bag of shit," he whispered, his words belied by the tenderness in his voice.

***

Brent parted his cracked, dry lips as if to speak, but couldn't seem to find the strength to form words. All he could manage was a soft moan. His body was tortured, the drugs only touching the tip of the iceberg of pain that he felt. He didn't remember much of what had happened – only snippets of memories, almost as if it had happened to someone else. The laundry room; lying on his back, his hands tied; the bolts of white-hot agony as he was dragged over the road. Not that any of that mattered. The only thing that mattered to Brent at the moment was that the first face he saw upon opening his eyes was Jake's.

"I was coming to tell you that I wanted to go with you, Brent," Jake whispered. "This is all my fault. All of it. You must hate me and I don't blame you a lick. I'm going to get them for you, Brent. They're going to pay for what they did. I swear it."

Brent's eyes misted with more than the pain. He tried to shake his head, tried to tell Jake that he didn't hold him responsible, but he couldn't move. "No," he managed to croak out in a voice so soft and breathy that Jake understood him only by reading his lips. A tear trickled from the corner of Brent's eye from the effort. "Not. Your. Fault." His eyelids began to flicker as he fought to remain conscious.

Jake sniffed, shaking his head. "Never you mind that now, anyway. Hey, you asked me to

go with you, remember? Don't you be going
nowhere without me, you hear? We got ourselves a deal."

The corners of Brent's lips curled up in a
brief smile, despite his pain and drug-induced
sleepiness, but a heartbeat later his eyelids fluttered and drifted closed again.

Wiping his eyes with his sleeve, Jake settled back in his chair.

***

Brent's parents arrived with the dawn of
the next morning. Carl Miller was an older
version of his son, his black hair streaked with
gray. His eyes were red-rimmed and his shoulders were stooped with worry under his navy
blue sports coat. The woman who clung to his
arm was salon-coiffed and polished, a slender
dark-haired woman dressed in a tailored silk
suit. Phyllis Miller wore the large, wrap-
around sunglasses of someone who'd recently
had cataract surgery, yet Jake was certain that
her eyesight was fine because when she spotted her son lying in his hospital bed covered in
plaster and bandages, her knees gave way.

Jake sprang up from his seat and took her
arm from Mr. Miller, nearly carrying Brent's
mother as he helped her to the chair. She
clutched a handkerchief to her mouth with one
hand, but patted Jake's hand with the other.
Carl Miller stood silently next to Brent's bed-

side, unmindful of his own tears as he gently touched his son's bruised face.

"He woke up last night for a couple of minutes," Jake said softly, wanting to give the Millers some kind of comfort. "Doc says every day his chances get better." He picked his hat up from the bedside tray, holding it in his hands and staring down at it.

Now that Brent's family was there, Jake felt like an intruder. He took a last look at Brent, then turned to leave to allow his parents some time alone with their son.

"Jake…"

Brent's voice was not much more than a ghost of a whisper, but it sounded like thunder in Jake's ears and froze him in his step. Turning, he saw that Brent's eyes were open and trained on him.

"Not. Without. Me."

Jake smiled, knowing what Brent meant. "I ain't going nowhere without you," he replied. "I done told you last night that we had ourselves a deal, remember? Works both ways."

"Stay."

Nodding, Jake settled back, leaning against a wall, his eyes never leaving Brent. "I'm a-waiting, Brent."

Brent's parents fussed over their boy, his mother crying and telling him over and over how much she loved him, and his father grimly pronouncing that they would see whoever had done this found and punished. Carl Miller sniffed loudly, then looked over at Jake.

"Do you know who did this?" he asked.

"No, sir… but I aim to find out."

"You let me know the minute you hear anything, understand?"

"Yes, sir."

Brent's mother took her turn addressing Jake, and as usual with mothers, it was on a much more personal note.

"Have you and Brent been friends for long, Mr. Goodall?" she asked, wiping her nose with her handkerchief. "Are you in the computer business, too?"

"No, ma'am," Jake answered truthfully, although he felt as though he'd known Brent forever. "We only met a few days ago."

"Oh," she replied, sounding disappointed. "I see. We were told that you were the one who got him to the hospital in time. He owes his life to you. Thank you for staying with him, Mr. Goodall. We're grateful that he wasn't alone," she added, a note of dismissal in her voice.

Jake nodded, but made no move to leave.

Carl Miller looked hard at Jake for a moment, saw how he in turn was looking at Brent and understood immediately what had happened between the two men. He merely looked at Jake, but the atmosphere in the room suddenly turned frosty.

"Dad," Brent whispered. "Don't. Not Jake's fault."

"No? Are you going to tell me that some gay-bashing homophobic bastard didn't do this, or that they didn't focus on you because of him? You nearly got yourself killed over some one-night stand!"

"Carl!" Brent's mother admonished, her eyes widening.

"No. Not Jake's fault. Love him," Brent answered, and Jake could tell he was fighting the pain and the drugs to stay awake and make himself understood. "Not his fault."

Jake face reflected the same astonishment as Brent's father at Brent's sudden confession. He was no more astounded by the words themselves than by Brent's willingness to say them out loud in front of his parents. He swallowed hard, feeling his cheeks burning.

Carl closed his eyes and ran a trembling hand through his hair. "I apologize, Mr. Goodall. Of course it's not your fault. I expect that you've had to deal with people who are capable of things like this all the time."

"It's Jake, Mr. Miller, and you were right. It *was* my fault. If it weren't for me, nobody would've taken much notice of Brent. He'd have been there and gone in one piece," Jake answered softly, his ragged emotions reflected in his voice. "I should've protected him, but I didn't... I couldn't. I knew better, but I..."

"No!" Brent growled from the bed, almost managing to raise his head from the pillow.

Jake frowned fiercely and stepped away

from the wall pointing a finger in Brent's direction. "You stay put, else I'll tie your ass down! You been through enough without making matters worse by getting yourself all riled up."

Phyllis smiled for the first time since walking into the room. "You listen to Jake, Brent. No one blames him, not me and not your father. And you, Jake Goodall," she continued, shaking her own finger, "are the reason that my son is still alive. The only ones at fault for this are the ones who hurt my baby. I don't want to hear another word from your mouth to the contrary, do you understand?"

Jake nodded, not convinced but unwilling to argue over it in front of Brent. While his stomach still churned with guilt, his mind was whirling over Brent's declaration of love. He didn't know if it was the drugs that had made Brent say it, whether he'd really meant it, or had even known what it was that he was saying. What Jake did know was that he would remember those words until his dying day.

***

Over a week had passed since Jake had last been home. He'd been showering and shaving in the bathroom of Brent's hospital room and sleeping in the chair at Brent's bedside. After a full week, the doctors had declared that Brent would not only survive, but that they were optimistic that he would recover fully from the beating. He still had a long, hard haul in front of him, but his chances were good. Jake had stood by silently as Brent's parents had both wept with relief, saving his own tears for the privacy of his truck.

Jake had spent the last week watching Brent's parents fret over their son, and had been surprised by their acceptance of himself in Brent's life. They had included Jake in their conversations and in their conferences with the doctors, and by the end of the week had been acting as though Jake were a part of the family. Being accepted in such a manner was, while completely alien to Jake, a warm and wonder-ful feeling.

As he watched him sleep, Jake thought that Brent had true courage the night his parents had arrived. He'd never once tried to hide who he was, and had made no bones about how he felt about Jake. Jake felt like a coward for forc-ing Brent to hide with him in the shadows, afraid of what others might think or do. If Jake had had the courage to be open about his feel-ings, had not been afraid of reprisals, then he would have spent that night at the motel room with Brent and he would not now be lying in a hospital bed. The guilt, although unspoken since that first night, still ate at him.

Sitting and watching Brent sleep and lis-tening to the beeps and buzzes of the ma-chines, Jake came to a decision. He had no intention of ever denying who he was again, regardless of the consequences. He would do that much in honor of Brent.

The next morning, he went home to face his own parents and tell them the truth. He stood in the parlor facing his father, his back ramrod straight and his eyes hard, staring at a spot on the wall over his father's head.

"So this the way it is, then?" Ray Goodall asked from his seat on the threadbare sofa. He picked at his fingernails, not able to meet his son's eyes. "I always suspected as much. What turned you, boy? What did me and your Ma do to make you this way?"

"You didn't do nothing, Pa. It's just the way it is, is all."

Jake's father fell silent again, his eyes never leaving his chipped and bitten fingernails. Finally, he nodded, then looked up at Jake.

"Be best if you didn't go back to that hospital, son. The ones that done this to that boy from New York, well, they ain't gonna stop if they find out you're still carrying on this nonsense with him. Nobody can prove nothing. It's our word against theirs that you was even with him."

"Let 'em come. I ain't afraid of nobody, Pa," Jake stated firmly. His eyes widened as he saw a guarded look cross his father's face. "You know who done this, don't you? You need to tell me if you do."

"Maybe. I got a visit from Joe Flynt night before last. He was talking about how that city faggot deserved to get messed up so bad, and how lucky he was to still be breathing. Said how lucky *you* was not to be in the same boat," Ray replied, shaking his head. "Told me if I was smart I'd tell you to quit chasing after bulls and get back to bedding heifers."

"The Flynt boys," Jake spat, the words tasting like vinegar in his mouth. "Shit, they're just the kind to go off and do something like this, ain't they? And I'll be goddamned if Billy himself ain't as queer as a three-dollar bill," Jake muttered, his fists balling at his sides.

"They ain't the only ones around here who feel that way, Jake. Don't you go off half-cocked now. I'll be telling the sheriff what Joe Flynt said if you stay away from that city man and you let the law take care of the Flynt boys," Ray replied gruffly. "Getting yourself killed ain't gonna help nobody. Best if you just get back to work at the store, and let this whole mess be. Things will get back to normal after a while… folks will forget."

Jake shook his head adamantly. "It's not going to be that way, Pa. I'm not staying in West Fork. When Brent gets well enough to travel, I'm going with him."

"What in the hell for?" Ray shouted, losing his temper at last and rising to his feet. "You're going to keep on being this way, and for what? You think they're going to let you ride in the pros knowing what you are?"

"What am I, Pa, besides being a damn fine rider? Anything else ain't nobody's goddamn business."

"You know what I'm talking about, Jake Goodall. Don't be smart-mouthing me, son. It could've been you lying in that hospital bed, instead of that stranger from New York."

"He's not a stranger to me, Pa. He means a lot to me."

"Don't let me hear you talking like that, Jake. Not in my own goddamn house! You need to forget this crazy shit and get back to normal! I ain't gonna watch them put you in the ground, son."

"Pa, this is the way I am. There ain't a choice to be made," Jake said, his face still hard but his gut wrenching. He feared what was coming, and it hurt. It hurt badly. "I spent my whole life hiding and I ain't fixing to keep pretending I'm somebody I ain't."

"What about us? What about the way folks look at your Ma and me at church on Sundays, or when they come around into the store, always whispering behind their hands? I hear what they're saying and so does your Ma. You ain't like this, Jake, not really. What about that Anders gal you was seeing a few years back?" Ray asked. "You was sweet on her, weren't you? Doesn't that mean that you ain't the way you say you are?"

"I only went with her to keep people from

talking about me, Pa. I never liked her that way… I never liked *any* girl that way and that's the God's honest truth. Pa, I'm gay. That's all there is to it. I ain't never gonna marry a woman, ain't never gonna give a woman children. I accept that now. You need to accept it too, else we're done here," Jake said simply, looking stonily at his father.

"Then we're done," Ray Goodall said, turning his back on his youngest son.

"I'm sorry, Pa," Jake whispered. He went to the door, looking back once, his eyes roaming over the room where he'd grown up as if to commit it to memory, then left and closed the door softly behind him.

His mother had never once come out of the kitchen.

***

Brent's parents had found it necessary to go back to New York after two weeks, and had left Brent's care in Jake's capable hands after eliciting a promise from Jake to call them each night with an update on Brent's progress.

"Don't forget to call us. Call collect if you need to," Carl said to Jake as they stood at the departures gate of George Bush Intercontinental Airport in Houston. They had ridden to the airport sitting three across in Jake's pickup, spending most of the three-hour ride in silence. The Millers were sorry to be leaving their son, while Jake was anxious to get back to him. "No, sir. I won't forget," Jake answered, manhandling their luggage out of the back of the pickup and placing it curbside.

"You have our numbers?"

"Yes, sir."

Phyllis took her turn as her husband fumbled for his identification and a tip for the skycap. "Don't let him give up, Jake. We're depending on you."

"Yes, ma'am.

Phyllis looked up at Jake for a moment then impulsively threw her arms around his neck, hugging him tight. "Brent is right about you, Jake Goodall. I can feel it in my bones. And if you don't start calling us by our names and desisting with this "sir" and "ma'am" nonsense, I'm going to fly back down here and beat you silly with your own ten-gallon hat!"

"Yes, ma'am… Phyllis," Jake replied, instantly correcting himself. He was a bit taken aback by her sudden show of affection, and was unsure of how to respond. He resorted to awkwardly patting her on the back.

He shook hands with Carl and had watched until they were safely inside the terminal before turning his clanking pickup around and heading straight back to the hospital.

Afterwards, he'd kept his promise, calling them that night and every night thereafter, faithfully, as soon as visiting hours were over. He continued to call them even after Brent had recovered enough to see to his own phone calls, growing closer to them and finding that he enjoyed their conversations.

Chapter Seven

In the weeks following the Millers' departure, Jake found himself busier than he'd ever been before, and at times pushed to the very limits of his endurance and patience.

The sheriff stopped by and had spent some time talking with Brent and Jake, asking them questions and jotting notes down in his spiral notebook. Brent told the sheriff about the older man at the rodeo who'd threatened him. Jake realized with a chill that Brent's description fit Joe Flynt perfectly. When the sheriff was through taking Brent's statement, Jake followed him out of Brent's room and told the officer of Jake's conversation with Ray Goodall.

"Your father got the impression from this conversation that the Flynt boys were behind this?" the sheriff asked.

"Yes, sir, he did," Jake answered, leaning back against the wall with his thumbs hooked into his front jean pockets.

"Any idea as to why Joe Flynt and his boys would be wanting to do this to your friend?"

"Yes, sir, I do."

The sheriff looked up from his pad. "And

would you care to share that information with me?" he asked, a bit sarcastically.

Jake looked the officer in the eye. "Because we ain't *just* friends."

Surprised, but only for a moment and covering it well, the sheriff nodded his head. "I see," he said, flipping his notebook closed. "Well, the problem we have here, Mr. Goodall, is that there ain't no witnesses and there ain't no evidence. Just your word against theirs, really, and that won't amount to a hill of beans in a court of law. It'd just be a case of he said, she said... or... well, you know what I mean. Still, we'll do the best we can."

With that half-hearted promise, the sheriff left. Jake was certain that the Flynt boys would never be charged, and there was a fair chance that he would have been correct if someone had not leaked word of what had happened to the press.

Not twenty-four hours had passed from the time of Jake's conversation with the sheriff that word reached the papers about the gay businessman from New York who'd been brutally assaulted in the small southwestern town of Stillwater. Although the reporter had not revealed the source of the story, Jake strongly suspected Carl Miller. He'd told Brent's father about Jake's meeting with the sheriff during his routine phone call the night before.

It was a hate crime, the reporters said, and Brent's picture had been plastered at first all over the newspapers out of Dallas and Houston, and then nationwide.

For a while they became the focus of a media circus as reporters and talk show producers repeatedly requested interviews with Jake and Brent. Some went to great lengths to speak with them, including one fellow from a supermarket tabloid who had disguised himself as a hospital janitor. Jake unceremoniously pitched him from Brent's room by the seat of his pants the instant he pulled his camera out from under his hospital greens.

But the pressure of the eyes of the nation being trained on Stillwater resulted in a more thorough investigation than Jake had expected. The FBI became involved when the sheriff indicated that he agreed that Brent had been targeted because he was gay. Eventually, the bartender at the Lobo came forward, giving a statement that revealed the details of a conversation he'd overheard at the bar between Joe Flynt and his sons on the very night of the attack.

The bartender's story, in addition to the reluctant testimony taken from Ray Goodall, was enough for a federal warrant to be issued for all three men. Joe Flynt and Cody Flynt were apprehended not two days later at the Lobo, led outside the bar, bloodied by deputies and charged with resisting arrest in addition to the charges of assault against and the attempted murder during the commission of a hate crime of Brent Miller.

Billy Joe Flynt was not present at the Lobo with his brother and father, nor did they give authorities any indication that they knew of his whereabouts. He remained at large, despite a massive manhunt launched by the authorities, including several stakeouts of his known haunts. Jake doubted if he'd be found. Billy had never been accused of being too bright, but Jake was certain that even *he* would have been smart enough to hightail it south of the border.

Flowers and cards arrived at Brent's hospital room by the truckload, some from friends and business acquaintances but most from people Brent had never heard of before. There were a few letters that made Jake's skin crawl when he read them, and he made certain that those made it to the trash before Brent ever saw them. Still, the ones that truly wished Brent well vastly outnumbered those few poison pen letters, and it made Jake realize that there were a lot of fine people in the world, restoring his faith somewhat in his fellow man.

***

Days melted into weeks, weeks into months. Brent's road to recovery was a long and difficult one, but Jake never once questioned his decision to stay with him, and the more time he spent with Brent the more certain Jake became that at Brent's side was exactly where he belonged.

The most difficult times came during the early weeks of Brent's physical therapy. Grueling hours spent working muscles and joints rendered stiff and weak by the attack took their toll on Brent, and he often snarled and snapped at Jake when he finally returned to his room, exhausted and hurting.

No matter how heated and irritated Brent became, Jake took it in stride, finding within himself a wealth of patience that never seemed to run out, and that he'd never known he'd possessed.

Just that afternoon Brent had lashed out again. He'd been wheeled back up to his room by his therapist, who looked pale and angry and had shot Brent a look to the back of the head that had warned Jake that Brent was in rare form.

"Don't fucking touch me!" Brent yelled as Jake moved to help him from his wheelchair and back into his bed.

"I ain't touched you yet!" Jake answered, then proceeded to do just that. He took hold of Brent's arms and pulled him up out of the wheelchair.

"What did I just fucking say?"

"I don't rightly know. Why don't you say it again?"

"I said not to fucking touch me!" Brent bellowed, trying to shake off Jake's hands.

"Sorry. I must be going deaf. Didn't hear you that time, neither," Jake answered, helping

Brent settle down onto the hospital bed. He lifted Brent's legs onto the mattress, then removed Brent's slippers.

"You must be deaf and stupid to boot!" Brent grumbled, moving his feet away from Jake's hands.

"'Scuse me? Did you say something about a boot? Like the one I'm goin' to kick your ass with if you don't settle down and let me help you?" Jake calmly replied, tucking the blanket around Brent as the man lay back on the mattress.

Brent scowled at Jake and rolled to his side, turning his back in a snit. "Kick *my* ass?" he muttered to himself. "Just wait until I'm back to my old self, then we'll see who'll be kicking whose ass."

Jake laughed. "I'll be looking forward to that day, partner. I'll even bend over to make it easier for you!"

Although he never said anything to Brent, it secretly pleased Jake when he was able to goad Brent into threatening him with what Brent thought he was going to do to Jake once he was healed. Much worse were the times when Brent refused to believe that he would *ever* be his "old self" again. Jake hated it when Brent sunk into a depressed funk, steeping himself in self-pity. After all he'd been through, Brent had every right to feel that way, Jake supposed, but it upset Jake to see him feeling so hopeless and he worried that Brent would give up.

"You need to leave, Jake," Brent said just a few days later, pulling the blanket up to his chin and averting his eyes.

"Visiting hours ain't over yet."

"You know what I'm talking about. Don't make this harder than it already is, Jake. Leave. Go home. Find somebody else."

"Now why on earth would I want to do that?"

"Jake, I'll still sponsor you, if that's what you're worried about, okay? But don't waste your life sitting around this fucking hospital room waiting for me to walk out of it, because it's never going to happen!"

"Don't piss me off, boy. You know that ain't why I'm staying," Jake answered, pulling the serving tray closer to the bed and removing the plastic lids that covered Brent's dinner. He pulled open the cellophane wrapper that contained a fork, spoon, knife, two sugar packets, and a napkin, and laid them out on Brent's dinner tray. "Now, look here," he said, "You got chicken tonight. Don't look half bad, neither."

"Damn it, Jake! I'm never going to get any better! Every fucking morning I get dragged down into therapy, where ham-handed sadists pull and prod and stretch me like fucking Gumby, and every afternoon I get sent back up here no fucking better than I was before. Why do you insist on staying with someone who's never going to be much more than a vegetable?" Brent whined, curling himself up into a ball.

"I like vegetables. Green beans especially, but I'm mighty fond of gourds, too," Jake replied, flicking the button on the remote that controlled the bed, lifting the head of the bed up so that Brent would be forced into a sitting position. "Like pumpkins, for example, or that big fat gourd that's sitting on the end of your neck." He began cutting Brent's dinner into bite-sized pieces.

"Goddamn it, Jake!"

In truth, Jake never considered leaving Brent, no matter how difficult things became for him. He found that no matter how trying a day he'd had, the time he spent in the evening with Brent – even when he was in a mood that could wilt a cactus - was worth it. To be honest, there were plenty of times when Jake, physically exhausted and emotionally drained, had wanted to crawl into bed next to Brent and not get up again, but leaving was an option that never once crossed his mind.

Jake's funds, meager to begin with, had quickly run out, forcing him to take work wherever he could find it. He practically lived out of his truck, continuing to shower and shave in Brent's hospital room and taking his evening meals in the little café in the hospital lobby. He worked mending fences or stocking shelves, doing odd jobs, anything that guaranteed a paycheck at the end of the week. But every moment that he wasn't working he could be found sitting in the chair next to Brent's bed.

It was during this difficult time that Jake received a message that had been left for him at the nurses' desk.

He hadn't seen or spoken with his mother and father since he'd declared the truth about his sexuality in the parlor of his childhood home. Their rejection had been a bitter pill to swallow, but the acceptance by the Millers and the happiness he'd found with Brent, regardless of his fluctuating moods, had gone a long way toward helping him bear it.

Still, he found himself unprepared when one of the nurses came into Brent's room and told Jake that his eldest brother had telephoned looking for him.

Joshua Goodall, married to his childhood sweetheart at the tender age of nineteen, had moved down to Houston where he'd found factory work. When Jake had spoken with him last, Josh and his wife had been expecting their fourth child in as many years, and he'd been promoted to floor supervisor at the factory. That had been nearly six months ago, well before Jake had met Brent Miller. That his brother would call him at the hospital meant that not only did Josh know about the circumstances that had brought Jake there, but also that whatever news he had to impart was grave.

Jake waited until after visiting hours were over before leaving Brent's hospital room and heading down to the lobby to find a payphone. He nervously dialed his brother's cell phone number, already knowing in his heart what the news was that his brother needed to tell him. The line rang on the other end, and a familiar deep voice answered.

"Josh? It's Jake."

"Jake, it's been a while, ain't it? You all right?"

"Yeah, Josh, I'm fine."

There was a pause, then Josh said, "I got some bad news, Jake. Real bad."

"Which one, Josh?"

"Pa. Just this morning, Jake."

Jake fell silent for a few moments, as his brother confirmed his fears. "How'd it happen, Josh?"

"Doc says it was a heart attack. He was sitting at the table and just keeled over, Ma says. He went right quick, didn't suffer none."

"Ma okay?"

"Holding up, so far," Josh answered. "The services are tomorrow, Jake. You got to come home."

Jack paused, thinking about his last visit home. "You know about what happened, Josh?"

"Yeah, bud. I know. Been all over the news down here."

"I went back to see them after it happened. Pa said we were done, Josh. Ma never even came out to talk to me."

"That may be, but it was hard on her, too, Jake. She's always had a hard life, and now she's alone. You were the last one of us to leave home. Losing Pa ain't gonna be easy on her," Josh said. "She needs her boys now, *all* of 'em, including you. Maybe even *especially* you, Jake. You're her baby boy."

"Her *gay* baby boy."

"That don't make no never mind. You're a member of this family, just like always. Come on home, Jake."

Jake closed his eyes and swallowed hard, not certain if it was acceptance or merely resignation that he heard in his eldest brother's voice. "All right, Josh. I'll be there."

He hung up the phone and walked back up to Brent's room, uncaring that visiting hours were over. One look at the grief on his face was enough to tell the nurses to leave him alone.

***

"Jake?" Brent asked when he sat on the chair and folded his arms up on the side of Brent's bed, burying his face in them. He took off Jake's hat and stroked his blond hair. His stomach clenched, knowing something had affected Jake badly for him to have silently laid his head on the side of the bed. "What's wrong? What's happened?"

"Pa had a heart attack," Jake's muffled voice replied. "He's dead, Brent."

Brent could hear a mixture of grief and anger in his voice, even though Jake kept his face hidden in the crook of his arm.

"Oh, no. I'm so sorry, Jake," he said softly.

For a long while Jake said nothing, keeping his face buried in his arms as Brent lent him his silent support, knowing Jake would speak when he was ready.

"I was pissed at him, Brent. I hated that he never once believed in me, and then hated him more for not accepting me and turning his back on me when I went to tell him how things were between you and me. He was a cold bastard sometimes. I'm even more pissed at myself for never telling him so and just taking what he gave me.

"But I guess I still kind of hoped we'd patch things up someday, you know? That's not going to happen now, not ever."

"Sometimes it happens that way, Jake, and there's nothing you can do about it. It was his decision, not yours. You shouldn't blame yourself for it."

"Maybe. He wasn't all bad, you know, except for over this and the rodeo. He was wrong about that, Brent, but he always did right by us while we were growing up. He was a good father when we were young. Worked hard, always got us what we needed. Never went hungry a day in my life and always had a roof over my head."

"I know, Jake. I know."

"I have to go home tomorrow for the funeral. I have to face my mother and my brothers."

"I'll go with you. One day out of here won't kill me."

"Oh, no, you're not. You're stayin' put. I ain't gonna chance you going against the doctors' orders by leaving the hospital and maybe getting yourself hurt worse. Besides, I think I need to do this on my own, anyhow," Jake said, lifting his head to turn sorrow-filled eyes to Brent.

Brent felt Jake's grief as if it were his own and opened his arms. Carefully crawling up over the mattress, Jake laid his head on Brent's chest and wept, his fingers wrapped tightly in the thin material of Brent's hospital gown.

***

Jake stood quietly, shoulder to shoulder with his three of his four brothers, their hats in their hands. Josh stood just in front of him, supporting their mother as the Goodall boys watched their father's coffin lowered into the dusty ground of the tiny cemetery. The mournful strains of "Taps" filled the air, played by a member of Ray's V.F.W. post. No one moved or spoke until the last wavering note had finally faded away and the silence had returned. Jake's mother clutched the American flag that had recently covered her husband's casket but was now tightly folded into a white-starred blue triangle, to her chest.

When it was over, Josh led Mae Goodall back to the waiting cars, followed by the rest of Jake's family, the women herding the children like sheep up the path toward the road. Josh looked back over his shoulder at Jake, who stood staring down at their father's grave. Jake nodded to him, hoping his brother would understand his need to pass a last word with their father in privacy. Josh nodded back before seeing their mother into his car.

After the small group of mourners left, Jake continued staring down at the flower-strewn casket that held the body of his father, lost in the memories of his youth. For all of the bitterness of their last parting, their lives had not always been at odds. Although Ray had often been busy working long hours at the feed store, Jake still had many happy memories of his father from when he was younger. He remembered his fifth birthday, when Ray Goodall had presented Jake with his first pony, a dappled gray filly. Another, a few years later, when Ray had taken Jake on a fishing trip along the Neches, just the two of them. Jake remembered the time he'd come down with the chicken pox, and his father had brought him a stack of comic books, sitting at his bedside as Jake read them aloud to him.

The last memory he recalled was the look on Ray Goodall's face as he had turned his back on Jake.

After a few minutes Jake squatted down next to the rectangular hole in the dry packed dirt of the cemetery.

"I'm sorry it ended the way it did between us, Pa. You were a stubborn old goat, and you were wrong this time, and that's the pure honest truth. *What* I am don't change *who* I am, Pa. It doesn't make me less of a man. Brent taught me that. He's a strong one, Pa. Stronger than me, I reckon, even if he is a city boy. You'd have liked him if you'd given him a chance." Jake sighed and stood up, setting his hat on his head. "You said a lot of things that hurt me real bad, Pa, but I'm not going to hold them against you. You did the best you could. Rest well, Pa."

He tipped his hat toward the coffin, then turned and walked back to his pickup. He'd made his peace with his father. Now he needed to try to make things right with his mother.

Chapter Eight

There was a flurry of activity in the old Goodall homestead, as neighbors and church friends of Ray Goodall stopped by to pay their respects to his widow. Each came laden with a covered dish, laying them out on the square, wooden kitchen table. Platters of fried chicken, green bean casseroles, baked beans, salads, biscuits, and pies were spread out, alongside stacks of paper plates, napkins, and plastic cutlery. Piled on the counters near the sink were enough covered casserole dishes and apple brown betties to feed all of West Fork for a month.

The hallway, kitchen, and parlor of the house were packed with people; so many that they spilled out across the porch and into the front yard. The rooms were filled with the steady hum of voices as neighbors and friends chatted with one another in quiet voices. Every so often a child would shriek as they chased one another around – and sometimes in between - the legs of the adults, blissfully innocent of the finality of death.

In the parlor, Mae Goodall, in a plain black dress, her narrow shoulders covered by a gray

sweater, sat on the old brown velvet sofa surrounded by four of her sons. Jake was the only
one missing, thinking it best to keep his distance for the time being. He sat just outside of
the kitchen door on the stoop, staring out at the
barn and the corral.

"Y'all need to come inside, Jake. Ma's
wondering where you got off to," Josh said,
opening the screen door and looking down at
his youngest brother.

"I don't want to be inside with all those
people in the house, Josh. Ain't no time to be
setting tongues to wagging, not with Pa just
put in the ground."

"She's asking for you, Jake."

Jake stared down at his hands. "You know
what happened, Josh. Everybody in the house
knows what happened to Brent and me. I'm
not going to pretend he doesn't mean a lot to
me. I'm not going to pretend to be somebody
I'm not anymore."

"Who you are is Mae Goodall's youngest
boy, and that's all you need to be, today. Come
inside."

Looking up into Josh's face, Jake saw the
concern in his big brother's cornflower blue
eyes. Josh had been more of a father to Jake
than Ray had been most of the time. His father
had been busy running the feed store more often than not, and it had been Josh who'd taught
Jake to ride the filly Ray had given him, who'd
thrown balls with Jake on the sun-baked field

behind the house, and later, had taught Jake to drive on the ancient, sputtering John Deere tractor. He'd been the one to defend Jake in schoolyard tussles until Jake had been old enough and strong enough to defend himself, and then Josh had been the one who saw to the inevitable bruises and bloody noses that had followed, helping Jake hide the evidence of a fight from their mother.

It had been Josh who'd taken Jake to his first rodeo, and had set him on his first calf. When Jake had ridden his first bull in competition, it had been Josh who'd been there to dust off his pride when he'd been bucked off, and who had encouraged Jake to keep riding.

Knowing that his brother hadn't turned his back on him after Jake's private life had been plastered all over the six o'clock news meant a great deal.

"What about you, Josh? Are you going to give me up for dead once this is all over?"

"Why? You plan on doing something stupid like letting a bull step on your melon-head?"

"You know what I'm talking about, Josh."

Josh stepped through the door and sat down on the stoop next to Jake. He took a pack of Marlboros out of his shirt pocket, shaking out a cigarette. Slipping it between his lips, he lit it with a battered, silver-cased Zippo, and sat smoking for a few moments before answering.

"I've always *known*, Jake. This whole thing ain't no big surprise to me. Can't purt near raise somebody and not know something like that about him. You remember the night I caught you rolling around in the hayloft with Betty Sue Anders?" he asked Jake.

Jake nodded, looking confused. "Yeah, you sure was in a sore state over that."

"I was only pissed 'cause it seemed to me that you were wasting a fine piece of ass up there, considering the way I used to see you looking at her brother, Bobby."

"How come you never said anything?" Jake asked, flushing scarlet. He was floored that his brother had seen through him so easily, guessing at what Jake had thought was his closely guarded secret, and a little embarrassed that he knew that Jake had had a crush on Bobby Anders.

Josh shrugged, then flicked his cigarette far out into the dirt. "Figured you'd say something when you were ready. Come on, now. Ma's a-waitin' on us."

Jake stood up and put his hand out for the handle of the screen door, but Josh stopped him for a moment.

"He good to you, this New York City fella?" Josh asked, not quite meeting Jake's eyes.

"Yeah, Josh. Real good."

Josh nodded, then opened the door allowing Jake to precede him inside the house.

The sky was streaked with reds and oranges by the time the last of the guests had said their goodbyes to Mae Goodall and her family. Not one of them had said a word to Jake about his recent troubles, although he'd felt his neck burn with the looks that had been tossed his way out of the corner of people's eyes. Several times a conversation had been stopped cold when he'd passed by, and he knew that he and Brent had been the topic of discussion.

Reverend Lucas McGraw, a white-haired scarecrow of a man in a turn-around collar, had given him withering looks the entire afternoon as Jake had stood stoically in the parlor, leaning against the fireplace mantle, staring down at his boots.

When at last he was alone with Jake and his family, Reverend McGraw approached Jake, cornering the cowboy in front of the fireplace.

"I've known Ray Goodall and his wife purt near all their lives, and I've known you, Jake Goodall, for all of yours. There ain't no greater sinner in the eyes of God than the unrepentant one, Jake Goodall. All this what's happened here is a punishment. That boy from New York's been judged, and I can see God's hand moving against you next, Jake. You done brought evil into our community, and He's fixing to…"

Josh's strong hand caught Reverend

McGraw by the elbow and pulled the man, sputtering in indignation, out of the parlor and out through the front door, all but flinging him onto the porch. Jake watched with mild interest as Josh did what he'd always done: protect his baby brother.

Reverend McGraw would never knew how close he'd come to being pitched out head first through the parlor window by the seat of his holier-than-thou pants, but Jake had seen it coming up fast and was glad that Josh thought to spare the family the expense of replacing the window panes.

Herding his brothers, their respective wives, girlfriends, and children out of the parlor and into the kitchen to deal with the mess that the mourners had left behind, Josh left Jake alone with their mother.

Still sitting on the couch, looking small and fragile, Mae Goodall kept her red-rimmed eyes cast down on the battered Bible she held on her lap. She had said very little during the wake, and nothing at all when Josh had virtually thrown the Reverend out of the house. Her silence made Jake wonder.

Sitting down on the far edge of the sofa, Jake set his hat on the coffee table and felt distinctly uncomfortable. He didn't know what to say to his mother. He knew how deeply religious she was, and for her to hold her tongue was surprising to Jake. Wanting to talk to her, but not sure of how to begin, he sighed deeply, fiddling with the snap at the cuff of his sleeve. To his surprise, his mother spoke first.

"I'm sorry, Jake," his mother whispered, lifting her eyes to look at her youngest son.

"You don't have anything to be sorry for, Ma," Jake replied. Although he did feel that she had reason to apologize, he saw no need to give her any more grief that day.

"Yes, I do. Last time you were here, I wanted to come out and talk to you. Wanted to tell you what I was feeling and get it over and done with, but I didn't. I was scared, Jake. Scared that you'd walk out and never come back any more. I was afraid that I'd say things that a mother shouldn't ever say to her son. Now, I'm real glad that I didn't have my say."

"Ma..."

"Let me finish, son. I don't pretend to understand all this, or why it is that you want to be with that New York fella instead of finding a nice girl and settling down. Reverend tells us that what you been doing is wrong, that you're paving your own way to eternal damnation. Your Pa believed it as much as I did.

"But what those Flynt boys did was more than just wrong. Reverend didn't say a blessed word about that, though. Truth be told, he held a service praying for them when Cody and his pa got arrested. Imagine, those boys beat your friend near to death for no reason other than being with you, and here's the preacher praying that they shouldn't go to prison for it. Said that God had been working through them, and that they shouldn't be punished for doing what they done.

"That's when I started thinking about that New York boy suffering up in the hospital, and how it could've been you just as easy as him. You never hurt anybody, Jake, not once in your whole life, and I'm willing to bet that that New York man never did either. What those Flynt boys did was done out of pure blind hate.

"Funny thing is that I was always taught that God didn't hold much with hate. That's when I realized that it wasn't His hand moving in this at all. Reverend McGraw was wrong.

"I guess what I'm trying to say is that God doesn't make mistakes, Jake. If this is the way He made you, then this is the way you're supposed to be. I'm sorry I didn't understand that sooner, and I'm sorry your Pa never understood it," Mae finished quietly, her shoulders trembling as she began to weep again.

Jake slid across the sofa and pulled his mother into his arms. His cheeks were wet with tears that had begun to fall during his mother's heartfelt apology. Her words meant more to Jake than he could say, and he stammered his feelings through his tears as he held her.

"Don't cry, Ma. It's okay. You and Pa, you always did right by me growing up. I love you, Ma," he whispered, kissing the crown of her head. "Thank you."

She sniffled, wiping her nose with a lace-trimmed handkerchief, then patted his hand. She pulled away to look up at him. "You bring that boy around here when he's feeling up to it, Jake Goodall. I got an apology waiting for him, too."

"I will, Ma. I promise."

***

The Reverend Lucas McGraw lived in three tiny rooms adjacent to the Victory Baptist Church, a whitewashed adobe building on the town's main street. Sitting in his favorite easy chair in his small parlor, Reverend McGraw looked steadily at the man who paced in front of him.

"Best if you just sit yourself down, Billy. Ain't nobody knows that you're here, and I ain't gonna turn you in," he said. "You get any word on your brother or your pa?"

"No, I ain't heard nothing, only that they're fixing to take them up to Dallas."

Reverend McGraw shook his head sadly. "Don't know what this world is coming to, when the law keeps good men like Joe and Cody Flynt behind bars and lets evil-doers like Jake Goodall and that New York man walk free. Ain't right, I say. The devil's come to roost in West Fork, Billy. Even Jake's brother Josh, who's always been a good man, done threw me out of his Pa's house. Ain't right."

"That whole family is tetched. Something's wrong with each and every one of them, except maybe for Ray, and he's dead. I shouldn't have listened to Pa. I should've went after Jake, instead of that city faggot."

"What are you gonna do now, Billy? You can't stay around here, not with the sheriff and the FBI lookin' for you, and your face being on the TV every ten minutes."

Billy Joe Flynt continued to pace across the small parlor, ten paces taking him from wall to wall. "I'm going to go out to that fishing cabin my Pa built out on the Neches. Nobody knows about that place except me, Cody, and Pa. Shit, it ain't much more than a couple of old boards and a tin roof, but it's hid real good. I'll lay low for a while, let things simmer down some."

"Then what?"

"Then I'm going after Jake Goodall, that's what. I ain't gonna rest till he's paid for this, Reverend. It's his fault my brother and my daddy are facing prison. After that, maybe I'll head south, cross the border. But I'm not going to rest until I see Jake Goodall dead."

***

Brent's depression eased and finally disappeared after he reached the point in his therapy where he began to make significant progress. Despite his own continuing pain and struggles, it was Jake that Brent remained concerned about, telling Jake that he was working too hard and got too little rest, and that he shouldn't be spending all of his free time sitting in a hospital room. No matter how many times Brent offered to pay Jake's way, he refused to take the money, insisting that he was doing fine. Brent complained that Jake was beginning to look haggard and was losing weight.

"You're going to whittle away down to nothing, Jake. You're not eating right, I can see it," Brent said, as he sat in a blue bathrobe on the side of the hospital bed. His casts had been removed just the day before, and his walker stood nearby. He was showing improvement every day and it wouldn't be long before he would be released from the hospital. "I don't think you've had a single decent night's sleep since that night we went camping."

"I'm fine. Quit nagging on me. You're worse than an old woman. Besides, you're the one who needs to chow down. I swear I can see your back through your front!" Jake retorted.

Brent reached up and ran his fingers over the scar that zigzagged in a lightning bolt pattern along the side of his head. "You never gave up on me, Jake. Why? I know for a fact that it couldn't have been easy for you. I've told you to go on home, but you never left.

You've been living out of your truck, not eating right, not riding, and there were times when I've said some nasty things to you, but you never said a word back. You just took it. Why?"

Jake smiled, then stood and walked over to the bed. Settling himself down next to Brent, he carefully put an arm around his shoulders, pulling him in close. "So you said a few things you didn't mean when you were in pain. It ain't like I've never been yelled at before. Shit, I've been known to cuss worse than a sailor on shore leave myself when I get bucked hard off a bull."

"You're avoiding the question, Jake. Why didn't you leave me?"

"You know why."

"If I knew why then I wouldn't be asking."

"Goddamn it, Brent-"

"I need to hear it, Jake. Please."

Jake sighed, then placed his hand on Brent's cheek, rubbing his thumb over the stubble that shadowed it. "You probably don't remember, but when you first woke up while your parents were here, you said something. Maybe it was the drugs talking, and maybe it was something you didn't mean to say, and that's why I never brought it up again. But it's the reason I stayed all this time."

Brent chewed his lip, trying to recall what it was that he'd said, but everything that had happened during the first few days after "the incident" (as he'd come to refer to the night he'd been beaten, dragged and nearly killed) had blurred into a foggy haze of pain. Suspecting what it might have been, he looked questioningly at Jake, silently urging him to continue.

"You said that you loved me," Jake whispered, still gently stroking the side of Brent's face with his fingers. "I ain't saying that you meant it, just that that's why I stayed. Because whether or not you meant what you said, hearing it made me realize that I was falling in love with you."

"You love me?" Brent asked, swallowing hard.

"Yeah, I reckon I do."

"You mean more to me than anyone I've ever known, Jake. I owe you more than I can ever hope to repay, and I'm grateful for everything you've done but that doesn't account for how I feel about you. I think I knew it from that very first night we were together on the bank of that river. If I said it, then it's because I meant it. I love you, too."

The door to Brent's hospital room happened to be closed, but they wouldn't have cared if it had been wide open and television cameras had been recording every move that they made. Jake's hand remained on Brent's cheek as he leaned in and kissed Brent softly, their first real kiss since the attack. Long, slow, and utterly tender, it was a kiss that wasn't charged with sexual energy as their previous kisses had been, but instead filled with the wonder of new love.

When their kiss finally ended, Jake's arms folded around Brent, holding him as close as he could without hurting him. Brent leaned his head against Jake's strong shoulder, a fragile smile playing at his lips.

"That door got a lock on it, Jake?" he whispered, lifting his head up and kissing Jake on his jaw.

"You ain't in no condition for what you're thinking, Brent Miller," Jake answered sternly, a curious combination of a frown and a smirk on his face as he pulled back and looked at his lover. "Your whole body was done busted up."

"There's at least one part of me that wasn't busted up."

"Yeah, and it's the *only* part that wasn't tore up. The rest of you is still healing."

"I need you, Jake."

"Brent, I don't even have any rub-"

"I *need* you. Now. *Please*."

Jake looked at Brent like there was nothing he would refuse him, not even if he had asked the cowboy to strip naked, paint himself blue, and run down the streets of Dallas singing *The Star Spangled Banner*. He looked deeply into Brent's eyes for a moment, then silently rose and went to the door, twisting the lock and sliding the bolt into place.

Stopping at the shelf near the bathroom

that held medical supplies, Jake fished out a couple of packets of lubricant from a box, grabbed a towel from the narrow closet, and tossed them onto the foot of Brent's bed.

Brent's breath came a little faster as he watched Jake slowly disrobe. First pulling off his boots and socks, Jake shimmied out of his jeans, and slipped his shirt from his shoulders, until he finally stood in nothing but his jockey shorts. By the time Jake's thumbs hooked into the waistband of his jockeys, Brent was nearly panting. Beneath his bathrobe, his cock had come roaring to life for the first time in months.

"Lie back on the bed, Brent. I'm not going to chance you hurting yourself by getting too rowdy," Jake ordered, carefully pushing Brent backwards. Just as he had that first night they had been together while camping out by the river, Jake peeled back Brent's blue bathrobe, unveiling his body. The barest traces of discoloration, faded to a sickly yellow, marked the places where Brent's body had been brutalized, and his scars had healed to shiny pink and white lines, a jigsaw puzzle remembrance of his pain.

Climbing onto the bed and straddling Brent, Jake picked up the packets of lubricant and tore them open with his teeth. He squeezed their gooey contents into the palm of his hand, then tossed the empty packets to the side.

Brent tried to spread his legs to open the

way for Jake to enter him, but Jake's knees squeezed together, preventing Brent from moving his lower body.

"Set still," Jake ordered, reaching between them and taking Brent's cock into his greased hand. With long, slow strokes he caressed Brent's hot flesh, until Brent fisted his fingers in the sheets of the bed and moaned softly.

After months of moaning in pain, *these* moans were music to both their ears.

Brent's eyes opened wide when Jake reached around himself and probed between his own cheeks. The look on Jake's face told Brent what he was doing, but Brent didn't allow himself to really believe it was happening until Jake hoisted himself up over Brent's erection and slowly lowered himself down.

The tightness and heat of Jake's virginal ass were indescribable and quite possibly the most exciting and overwhelming experience Brent had ever had before in his lifetime. Coupled with the knowledge that Jake was doing this for him alone – trusting and loving Brent enough to give him a part of himself that he had never before given anyone – made it nearly too much to handle. He came almost immediately, filling Jake to overflowing.

Jake's hand was pumping over his own cock, but as soon as Brent came down off the high of his orgasm he smacked Jake's hand away with a growl. This much he would give back to his lover.

He pulled at Jake's hips until he inched his way up until his knees straddled Brent's chest. Uncaring that the rigid length before him was coated in lubricant from Jake's hand, Brent swallowed him whole, sucking hard and fondling the sac that hung below Jake's erection. Allowing a finger to slip back to massage Jake's perineum, Brent was rewarded with a long low moan from Jake.

Brent's talented tongue and hands helped Jake quickly forget the discomfort of having been breached for the first time. Bracing his hands against the wall behind the head of Brent's bed, Jake leaned forward, hungry for more contact. He gritted his teeth, holding back obviously trying to keep from plunging more of his cock into Brent's mouth than he was willing to take.

Brent slipped his hands behind Jake, kneading the clenching muscles of his ass. Slipping his fingers into the crack, Brent rubbed gently at Jake's lubricant-and-semen slicked asshole, then slipped a finger inside and probed for Jake's prostate.

With a loud cry that must have been heard outside the room at the nurse's desk, Jake came in hot spurts, his ass clenching tightly and his body trembling uncontrollably. Brent drank every drop, refusing to release Jake's cock until he'd licked it clean.

A sharp rapping at the door froze them both for a heartbeat, then set them both laughing. "No maid service today!" Brent called out cheerily, snickering against Jake's shoulder. Jake blushed scarlet, but still took the time to lean down and kiss Brent, tasting himself on his lover's tongue.

Rising from the bed, Jake carefully cleaned Brent and himself off, and dressed, resolutely ignoring the pounding and the threats being shouted out from the other side of the door. First making certain that Brent had once again covered himself with his bathrobe, Jake unlocked and opened the door to admit a scowling, furious older nurse.

She glared at the two of them, obviously wanting to dress them both down for horsing around in a hospital room and opened her mouth to do just that, but one look from the rough-looking cowboy was enough to make the words stick in her throat. Huffing, she turned on her sensible heels and stalked out again, her shoes making angry little squeaks across the tile floor.

Jake cracked a grin as soon as she left, then walked over and sat on the bed next to a chuckling Brent.

"Thank you," Brent finally said, when his laughter had subsided into hiccups and he had sobered. He leaned in for a kiss.

"Don't be thanking me. I'm the one that should be grateful, here," Jake said, shaking his head. "I got the better end of the deal with this one, Brent. You're the one that's getting the ass end of the bull with me."

Brent took hold of Jake's chin in a firm grip. "Don't ever let me hear you say that again, Jake Goodall. I can't even begin to match you. All I can hope for is that you'll know how much I love you, and stay with me."

"Just you try to get rid of me," Jake answered softly before pulling Brent into another long, sweet kiss.

Chapter Nine

New York City was nothing like Dallas. Here were canyons of concrete, each block so tightly packed with skyscrapers that a man had to lean back and crane his neck to catch a glimpse of the sky. The sky itself was more gray than blue, and there were no stars to be seen anywhere at night because they were outshone by the blazing lights of the city.

The lights fascinated Jake. Dallas had lights, of course, but not like this. Neon sizzled everywhere; bright white bulbs glowed over marquees and tiny, colorful chasing lights twinkled and sparkled around every store window. Strobe lights flashed, and fluorescent lights sputtered, streetlights glowed, and traffic lights blinked red, amber, and green. It was as if New Yorkers had taken the stars from the skies over Texas and used them to decorate their doorsteps. It was daytime even in the dead of night.

Brent's apartment was on the twenty-seventh floor of a building on 33rd Street, close to the skyscraper on Madison Avenue where his company occupied two entire floors. Jake had never seen anything like the apartment except on television, and he was almost afraid to touch anything for fear of breaking something valuable.

Brent's apartment was cavernous. His master bathroom alone was twice the size of Jake's entire trailer back home. The first night they'd arrived in New York, Jake had joked that Brent had better draw him a map or he'd likely get lost walking from the bedroom to the kitchen.

Paintings by artists Jake had never heard of provided bright splashes of color, gracing the walls in elegant frames that themselves were worth more than Jake had earned in a month working at the feed store. Statues, mostly nudes but also some that Jake couldn't quite figure out, stood on pedestals illuminated by soft spotlights.

Everything Brent owned seemed to operate at a touch of a button. The coffee table in the living room looked like an electronics store with all of the remotes that Brent had laid out on it, and each of them did something different. One operated the enormous big screen television, the VCR, and the DVD player. Another controlled the stereo system. Yet another dimmed and brightened the lights in the room, and still another opened and closed the vertical blinds that hung across the huge plate glass window. Jake's personal favorite was the small white remote. Pushing the blue button on *that* one caused a fire to crackle to life inside the hearth of Brent's freestanding fireplace.

Aside from the electronics, Brent's apartment was tastefully decorated in subdued blues and ivories. Parquet flooring and luxurious carpeting ran throughout it, complementing Brent's sleek modern furniture and glass-topped accessories.

Brent had told Jake that he was well off financially and that he owned his own computer software business, but Jake had had no clue of exactly what "well off" had meant until he'd seen Brent's apartment. Aside from offering to sponsor Jake on the pro circuit, Brent had never flaunted his wealth, nor had he ever once made a disparaging remark about Jake's much simpler lifestyle. Still, the fact that his lover was wealthier than anyone Jake had ever known personally didn't really faze him until Brent began buying him things.

The first gift had been a coat. Black leather as soft as butter, it had fit across Jake's shoulders as if it had been made for him alone, falling in pliant folds to his ankles. He'd protested at its obvious expense, but had accepted it and thanked Brent for his generosity.

A new wardrobe large enough to fill one entire side of Brent's huge walk-in closet swiftly followed the coat. Jackets, pants, jeans, and shirts in wools, linens, cottons, silks, hand-stitched and designer-labeled, and in every color of the rainbow, found their way into Jake's half of the closet. Shoes and boots in leather, snakeskin, and alligator hide came in a regular procession. It seemed a stack of new boxes appeared nearly every time Brent walked in through the front door.

The kicker, the point at which Jake had scowled and told Brent in no uncertain terms that enough was enough, came the night Brent had come home and handed Jake a small box that had *Tiffany & Co.* written on it in neat lettering. The box had contained a solid gold ring with a sapphire mounted in the center of it that looked big enough to choke a horse. Square-cut diamonds on either side surmounted the sapphire.

"No more, Brent," he said, shaking his head and putting the ring back into the little blue box it had arrived in. He pushed the box back across the glass top of the coffee table toward Brent.

"What's wrong? Don't you like it? It's your birthstone, a sapphire," Brent asked, looking concerned that Jake hadn't liked his taste in jewelry.

"I know what it is. I also know how much it must have cost. You're not buying anything for me any more, Brent. Not one more thing. You done bought me too much already. I feel bad enough that I haven't been pulling my weight around here without you throwing gifts at me every two seconds."

"Jake, don't be silly. We're together. You don't need to pull anything. What's mine is yours."

"No, we're together and what's yours is *staying* yours. I told you back in Texas that I don't cotton to charity."

"This isn't charity!"

"Feels like it."

Brent sighed and shook his head, then scooted along the couch to snuggle close to Jake, wrapping his arms around Jake's slender waist. "It's not charity," he repeated, more forcefully.

"I mean what I say, Brent. No more."

"Jake, I love you. It makes me happy to give you things."

"That might be, but it don't make *me* happy. I feel like a leech, Brent, living off you like I been, not working, not contributing anything. It ain't right," Jake said sternly, pushing Brent away and looking hard at the man. "I love you, too, but there's nothing more that I need, and I don't want you spending a single wooden nickel on me anymore."

Brent looked into Jake's eyes and saw that he was in earnest. "All right, Jake, if that's what you want. I'm sorry. I didn't mean to make you feel that way. I've just been so incredibly happy that I wanted you to be happy, too."

"I *am* happy, Brent," Jake said, relenting and pulling Brent back into his arms again. "I was happy sitting in front of that plain ol' campfire out by the river with you, and I'm just as happy sitting in front of this fancy electronic fire with you now. I don't need you buying me stuff to make me happy. *You* make me happy."

"What did I do to deserve someone as special as you, huh?" Brent whispered, lifting his head up toward Jake.

"Guess you just got lucky is all."

Brent smacked Jake playfully then leaned in to kiss him.

"I'm gonna look for work tomorrow, Brent," Jake announced when Brent allowed him to come up for air.

"I don't think that there's much call for bull riders in the city, Jake," Brent said, trying to recapture Jake's lips with his own.

"You're pissing me off, city boy," Jake growled. "I don't mean riding and you know it. I have a strong back. I can work anywhere doing anything that's needed."

"I know you could, Jake. Look, there really isn't any sense in you taking a job right now. We aren't going to stay in New York for long. I promised you that I was going to relocate to Dallas, remember? I meant it."

"I know what you said, but New York is your home. Your apartment is here, your business is here, your family is here, your friends are here. Your *life* is here," Jake said, shaking his head.

"My home is wherever I make it, Jake. As long as I'm with you, I couldn't care less if I were in New York, Dallas, or in the middle of the Antarctic," Brent replied, smiling. "Life has a way of throwing you a curve now and then, and people change because of it. I used to love New York and missed it the moment I left it. But since I've met you, you hardheaded mule, I find myself missing Texas instead. I enjoyed that week we spent at your mother's house more than any fancy vacation I've ever taken. I miss the stars, Texan, and I miss you naked underneath them."

"Brent?"

"Yes, Jake?"

"Shut up."

Jake had found he was becoming choked up over Brent's little speech, and covered his rush of emotions by pulling Brent closer for another long, deep kiss. He pushed Brent down onto the soft cushions of the sofa, and for a while the only sounds in the apartment were their soft moans and the crackling of the fire.

After a short while, Brent said, "Jake?"

"Yeah?"

"I have a confession to make. There is this one other thing that I bought-"

"Take it back," Jake ordered, sucking at the tender flesh of Brent's throat, making Brent wriggle underneath him.

"I can't, Jake. I bought it while we were staying at your mother's house in Texas. It's too late to do anything about it." Jake's fingers unbuttoned his shirt and his lips traveled down over his skin to his chest, drawing a moan from Brent.

"You never left my side when we were in Texas. When did you have time to buy anything?" Jake replied, his words muffled against Brent's skin.

"Well, actually, I had your brother, Josh, find it, and my lawyers conducted the purchase. I just paid for it."

"What?" Jake asked, surprised. He picked his head up from Brent's chest where he'd been lapping at a nipple, and narrowed his eyes. "What did you do, Brent Miller?"

"I bought us a ranch."

Jake pushed himself up off Brent and sat back, staring down incredulously. He opened his mouth, but for once in his life nothing came out.

Brent sat up, looking at Jake with worried eyes. Jake didn't say anything at all, and Brent was braced as though Jake would soon be yelling his head off.

"It's not a very big ranch, Jake, honest," Brent said, trying to head off an argument. "Just a little one, and I bought it before I knew how you felt about me buying things. I just wanted us to have somewhere to go when we relocated," Brent continued. He was rambling, the words flying out of his mouth in rapid-fire succession.

"I've bought a condo in Dallas, too, but I knew you would rather not live in the city.

Plus, Josh told me that you'll need to practice if you were going to enter the pro circuit, and you couldn't very well ride bulls through the streets of downtown Dallas. There's a bucking machine on order, too, but that doesn't count because it's a part of my sponsoring you…"

Jake reached over and clamped his hand tightly over Brent's mouth. "You bought us a ranch?"

Brent nodded his head, Jake's hand still firmly covering his mouth. He winced, preparing himself for the explosion he was certain was soon to come.

Suddenly, without warning, Jake gave a loud, whooping yell and threw himself at Brent, knocking him back down onto the sofa cushions. Jake was grinning from ear to ear as he bounced excitedly on top of Brent. "A ranch? An honest-to-God ranch? And it's all ours? Hot damn!"

"You're not angry?" Brent asked. He smiled widely at Jake's obvious delight and excitement.

"Shit, no! Is it a working ranch? Does it have livestock? What kind? Horses? Cattle? Sheep? How many acres?" Jake asked without pausing to take a breath. He was as excited as a little boy on Christmas morning, making Brent laugh. "We're going to need to hire hands to work it, I reckon."

"Cattle, and from what Josh tells me we've already got all the help we need working it, including him and his wife. He accepted the job as foreman, Jake. I hope you don't mind that I asked him-"

"Goddamn it, but I love you, Brent Miller!" Jake cried, crushing his lips to Brent's and eliminating any further need for explanations.

***

They were set to leave in a week's time. A mountain of boxes and crates had already been shipped out, some to the condo in Dallas and others to the ranch, leaving Brent's apartment looking bare and sterile. All that was left in it were a few pieces of necessary furniture, some of their clothing, and of course, Brent and Jake.

Brent had insisted that he wanted to bring something back with them for Jake's mother, something pretty, and had dragged Jake to Fifth Avenue to help him pick something out.

After Brent had been released from the hospital, and over Brent's protests, Jake brought him home just as he had promised his mother he'd do. Brent hadn't forgotten the cool reception he'd received the last time he'd been in Jake's childhood home, and hadn't been looking forward to the visit.

Brent found himself surprised however, by the warm welcome that he received from Mae Goodall, as well as the apology she offered the moment he'd set foot in her house. She'd cried, just as she had with her own son, which had made Brent teary-eyed, and both of them sniffling together had made Jake had clear his throat and look as if he might join them.

They'd stayed a week, helping with odd jobs around the house. Mae Goodall had been overly solicitous of Brent, chiding him for overexerting himself and dressing down Jake for allowing him to do so.

"You just got out of the hospital, Brent Miller. You got no call to be climbing up on the roof hammering at shingles. You want to help, then you just come down here this minute and sit by me. You can help me snap these beans," she had ordered, standing by the ladder with her hands on her hips. "Jake Goodall! You tell your fella to get his scrawny hide down here! What's wrong with you, boy? I swear, neither one of you has half the sense the good Lord gave you."

Brent had grinned at Jake, and had carefully maneuvered his way down the wooden ladder, happily sitting with Jake's mother on the doublewide porch swing, snapping beans into a white enamel basin.

Jake's three middle brothers, all of whom still lived in the immediate area, had taken over running the feed store and caring for their mother, for which Jake was grateful. It left Jake free to follow Brent to New York.

***

"Ma don't have a need for any of this fancy stuff, Brent. If you want to get her something then get her a new washing machine," Jake said as they passed window after window filled with trendy clothing and sparkling jewels. "And you can get *that* out of the Sears Roebuck catalog. Let's go home."

"Jake! You should be ashamed of yourself. Your mother has spent her entire life working her fingers to the bone in that house raising five boys. We are *not* bringing her a washing machine!" Brent replied adamantly, scowling at Jake. He stopped when he saw the smirk that creased Jake's cheek. "Oh, I get it. Giving the city boy a hard time, huh?" He elbowed Jake, then led him into Cartier's.

They settled on ordering Jake's mother a lovely heart-shaped pendant set with seven precious stones. The two largest, a ruby and an emerald, were suspended in the center and represented Mae and Ray Goodall's birthstones. The five gems that surrounded them were the birthstones of her five sons. Jake shook his head at the cost, but said nothing. This gift wasn't for him, after all.

A short while later, their purchase for Jake's mother concluded, the jeweler having promised that the pendant would be ready by the next day, Brent and Jake sat at an outdoor café sipping coffee. Jake had fallen silent, and

Brent noticed an irritated look cross his face. "What's wrong, cowboy?" he asked, putting his cup down in its saucer.

"People keep staring at me. Since I got to New York I've been feeling like I grew an extra head or something," Jake replied, shifting his body so that his back faced the sidewalk. "It's always like this, Brent. I wish they'd quit it. Nobody stares like this back home."

"It's the hat, buddy boy," Brent chuckled, reaching over and tugging on the brim of Jake's Stetson. No matter what function they had attended together, no matter how casual or formal the occasion, wherever Jake went, his cowboy hat followed. "Let's face it. You are one sexy cowboy."

Jake blushed crimson, and pulled the brim of his Stetson down lower over his eyes. "Think people never seen a cowboy before."

"Jake, if you ever gave up bull riding, you could be a model. You're a handsome man."

"So are you, but people don't stare at you like this."

"*I* look like a goddamn patchwork quilt, Jake," Brent said, his expression clouding for a moment as his fingers touched the scars on his face. He shook it off, grinning at the cowboy. "But you are absolutely gorgeous. I'm glad we're going back to Texas before some pretty young thing steals you away from me."

"Knock it off, Brent," Jake said softly, taking the man's hand in his. "Ain't nobody taking me anywhere, and I still think you're the prettiest thing I've ever seen. Thought so that first night in the Lobo, and I *still* think it." He gave Brent's hand a squeeze to emphasize his words.

Since arriving in the Big Apple, Jake had quickly gotten over his reticence in showing affection with Brent in public. After expressing shock at the open affection shown between gay and lesbian couples the first time Brent had taken him through Greenwich Village, Jake would often take Brent's hand as they walked the streets of New York, or would lean over for a kiss without even thinking about it. In New York, no one blinked an eye. In Manhattan, unlike West Fork, they were just another couple in love.

"You're going to make me cry in my cappuccino, Jake. Then people will *really* stare," Brent laughed, although his heart warmed at Jake's words. He knew that he remained self-conscious about the scarring that remained as a reminder of his injuries, and the truth of the matter was that he often seriously worried that Jake might wake up one day and find him repulsive. He'd never spoken to him about it because he knew what Jake's answer would be, but that didn't stop Brent from losing sleep over it from time to time.

"Are you finished?" Brent asked Jake, eyeing his empty coffee cup. "Let's go back home and relax for a while. We've been invited out tonight by a few friends, sort of a goodbye gala."

***

"Shit, not again," Jake mumbled, rolling his eyes. He'd found out soon enough that he didn't enjoy the New York City nightlife. Jake didn't care for dancing, and Brent could rarely pull him out onto the dance floor without having to hogtie him first. At the very best, Jake might allow Brent a couple of slow dances, but anything faster than a two-step was beyond his ability.

Jake also preferred a simple beer to the colorful, exotic drinks favored by Brent's friends, and on the rare occasion that he drank hard liquor, he'd rather it not be encased in Jell-O or drunk out of some stranger's belly button.

As a matter of fact, he found that he didn't have much in common with Brent's friends at all. Jake found most of them to be too plastic and shallow, too wrapped up in who was doing what with whom to be very interesting. Plus, most of them seemed too damned eager to touch him, and worse yet, to touch Brent. He'd never seen such a pack of kissy-huggy men before in his life. The first time one of them had thrown his arms around Brent's neck, hugged him tightly and had planted a kiss on Brent's lips, Jake had pulled Brent's friend sharply away and had nearly decked the wide-eyed man.

Still, Brent had done so much for him that Jake was hesitant to say no to anything Brent asked of him, especially when it was something as simple as going out to a club for the evening. He resigned himself to spending yet another night being bored to tears.

Six hours later found Jake as duded up as a groom on his wedding day, trussed up from head to tail in perfectly tailored Armani. With his old battered Stetson firmly planted on his head, he followed Brent into one of the trendiest clubs in the city, led past the velvet-roped line of hopeful club-goers that stretched all the way down the city block and around the corner.

Threading their way through the crowd of people inside the club, past the enormous steel and leather bar and skirting the jam-packed lighted dance floor, Brent led Jake to a large table set near the DJ's booth. As usual, as soon as Brent arrived he was inundated with hugs and kisses by his friends, who immediately extended their welcome to include Jake, much to his consternation.

The first round of drinks was quickly followed by a second and a third, while Jake sat nursing the same beer. Brent was on his fourth round when a short, stocky man, as bald as an egg and wearing enough gold to fill Ft. Knox wandered over, pausing to stand behind

Brent's chair. Jake noticed him, although Brent did not.

"I can't believe that you're serious about moving out into the godforsaken wilderness, Brent. What's out there in Texas besides cactus and cows?" a thin strawberry blond with a neatly trimmed goatee was saying.

"Cow*boys,* Alan!" interjected another of Brent's friends. He turned to Jake, flirting outrageously. "Are there more like you out there, Jake? If there are I might just have to move out there myself!"

"You wouldn't last a day out there, Jeff. The first time you missed a manicure, you'd be on a plane heading back here," Brent laughed, draining the last of his glass.

"They have salons in Dallas," Jeff answered a bit huffily. "Besides, why should you be the only one to hook a looker like your cowboy?"

"A bull-riding cowboy, no less!" laughed Alan. He sighed dramatically. "When I grow up, I want to be a bull rider!"

Jeff shook his head. "Not me. When I grow up I want to be the bull and get *ridden* by bull riders!" Mike guffawed and clinked glasses with Jeff.

"So, the rumor's true that you're moving to Texas, Brent. Is it because he rides a bull or because he's hung like a one?" the baldheaded man behind Brent asked snidely, snickering and casting a disdainful look at Jake. He put his hands on Brent's shoulders, massaging them.

"Knock it off. Leave me alone, Mike" Brent said, Turning his head and looking up at the baldheaded man and shrugging his shoulders free. "And leave Jake alone, too, while you're at it."

"Oh, aren't you so cute! I wouldn't have thought your big, strong cowboy would need someone to defend him. You know Brent, since you brought your new little pet home with you I've been hearing rumors that you were going to move to Texas. I just can't believe that you'd throw me over for this hayseed in bargain-basement Levis," Mike spat. It had been well known in their circle of friends that Mike had held high hopes of landing Brent himself - along with Brent's money - regardless of the fact that Brent would barely give the man the time of day.

"Grow the fuck up, Mike," Brent hissed. "You're a goddamn nutcase!"

"Don't be such a bitch, Brent," Mike snarled venomously. "Honestly, have you completely lost your senses since you took up with the Marlboro Man over there? You always go overboard with these new lovers. He's just a farm boy with a big dick, and you'll get tired of him soon enough, just like you always do. Then you'll come crawling back to me."

"You might just want to watch your mouth," Jake said in a deceptively calm voice.

Brent looked over, acknowledging that Jake was an inch and half a heartbeat away from plowing his fist into Mike's face.

"I was talking to Brent, not you, Roy Rogers. Did he tell you that we're lovers, cowboy? No, I'll just bet that he hasn't. He's told you that he loves you, though, hasn't he? Well, I have news for you - he says that to everybody, including me. Believe me, it doesn't mean a fucking thing to him."

"Shut the fuck up!" Brent bellowed, pushing Mike away from the table. "Don't listen to him, Jake. He's certifiable."

"Oh, sure, that's what you say now, Brent, but that's not what you said while you were fucking me last week," Mike grinned, perversely enjoying the look on Jake's face as it blanched white.

"That true, Brent?" Jake asked quietly. His entire body started to tremble with anger. Whether it would be directed at Brent or at Mike was yet to be determined, but *somebody* was going to get plowed under.

"You don't think he'd tell you the truth, now do you? I'd be afraid to if I were Brent. Look at you. You look like you're ready to kill someone," Mike laughed, even as Brent's friends rose up out of their chairs and began to drag him away from the table. "Come on, cowboy! He's using you for your cock! Did you really think that a man with Brent's education and money could *possibly* fall in love with somebody like *you*?" he called out as Brent's friends dragged him into the crowd. "You'll be gone the minute he gets bored with you!"

"He's crazy, Jake. Don't listen to him," Brent said, reaching up to cup Jake's cheek.

Jake pulled away, and looked Brent in the eye. "If it's true you need to tell me right now, Brent."

"How can you even *ask* me that? I wouldn't cheat on you, Jake!" Brent retorted, starting to get angry himself. He'd never given Jake any reason not to trust him, and he was annoyed that Jake would question his fidelity.

"That ain't what he says."

"*He* is a pathological liar who I slept with exactly once over a year ago, Jake. He's been trying to get back into my pants and my wallet ever since. I can't believe that I need to defend myself to you over this nonsense!"

***

Jake's mind was in an uproar. The possibility that Brent would want to sleep with someone else had never really crossed his mind before, not until just a few moments ago. But now he felt panic roiling in his gut.

"He said you and him were... Did you sleep with him, Brent? Is that what you've been doing when you said you were in meetings?" Jake asked, not hearing anything beyond the fact that Brent had indeed slept with

Mike once. Mike had hit upon Jake's vulner-
able spot with unerring accuracy, and once ex-
ploited, Jake's insecurity washed over him like
a tidal wave. How *could* he expect someone
like Brent to stay faithful to a simple cowboy?
Brent was educated, used to fine living and
had expensive tastes. Jake was most comfortable in a bunkhouse, and only bought new
jeans when his old ones got to the point where
they were more holes than fabric.

"How do I know what *you've* been doing
while I was at work? I trust you, Jake. It hurts
to know that you don't trust me."

"You didn't answer the question, Brent."

"I'm not going to answer it. It should never
have been asked in the first place."

Jake looked at Brent for a moment, his
mouth clamped into a tight thin line, then rose
and shouldered his way through the crowd,
ignoring Brent's voice calling him back.

By the time Brent was able to push his way
to the door, Jake was gone.

Jake wandered aimlessly for a couple of
hours after stalking out of the nightclub. His
mind was whirling, and he'd managed to
nearly convince himself that Brent had indeed
been carrying on an affair while Jake had sat in
his apartment, twiddling his thumbs. It oc-
curred to Jake that guilt might have been the
reason for Brent's lavish gifts, and an affair
would explain the frequent long hours Brent
had spent away from him under the pretense of

working. The more Jake thought about it, the more convinced he became and the angrier he got.

He turned into the next bar he came across, a seedy dive that smelled of booze and piss, and proceeded to drown himself in shots of Jack, beer back, flavored with generous doses of self pity.

***

Two days later, Brent sat in his office, a fifth of Scotch with two fingers left in the bottle sitting on the desk in front of him. He looked like shit and felt three times worse, having spent the last two days dividing his time with being frantic over Jake's disappearance and beating himself up over the way he'd handled the situation at the bar.

He'd phoned Jake's brother, Josh, hoping that he'd heard from Jake. He'd phoned Jake's mother, his own parents, and the police, and had done everything he could think of doing short of plastering Jake's face on milk cartons in an effort to find him. No one had heard from him, and the police had politely informed him that there was nothing they could do since Jake was an adult, and he and Brent had had an argument. There was no suggestion of foul play. It was Jake's right to disappear, if he wanted to do so.

Brent poured the last of the Scotch into his

glass, downing the fiery liquid in one long gulp. Setting the glass down, he rubbed his hands over his face. He couldn't concentrate on his work, not with Jake missing, but he couldn't bear to go home to his empty apartment, either. Every time he closed his eyes he saw one of two things. In his mind's eye Brent would see Jake in bed making love to someone else, or else he'd see Jake dead, lying inside a dumpster in a dark alley and, quite frankly, Brent didn't know which vision was worse.

A short tone sounded, indicating that Brent's secretary wished to speak to him. He was tempted to ignore her, but pressed the intercom button on his telephone. "I said to hold my calls, Sherry," he said tersely. "All I want to be disturbed for are the Oxford papers."

"I'm sorry, Mr. Miller, but Jake Goodall is here. I told him that you're not seeing anyone today, but he won't leave," his secretary replied. Brent could hear the irritation in her voice. "Should I call security?"

"No! Send him in!" Brent yelled, jumping up from his chair and quickly walking around the side of his desk.

The door opened and Jake walked in, holding his hat in his hands. If anyone looked worse than Brent did at that moment, it was Jake.

He looked like he hadn't eaten or slept in two days, and he'd had more than a passing acquaintance with liquor for most of those days.

He stood just within the door, as the secretary first shot a look at Brent and then at Jake, shook her head and closed the door. Jake continued staring at his boots, nervously moving the brim of his Stetson through his fingers.

"I'm about as sorry as a man can get, Brent. I had no call to run off like that. No call to doubt you," he said, never taking his eyes off his boots. "I was jealous, and that's a fact."

"No, it was my fault, Jake. I should've just answered you straight up. Jake, I haven't slept with anyone since I met you. I haven't wanted to, either. I never-" He stopped abruptly as Jake raised the palm of his hand up.

"Stop. It wasn't you, it was me. Seems to me like I keep fuckin' up, Brent. First, I damn near drowned you in the river, then I let you go and get beat on and nearly killed, and now this," Jake said, his mouth twitching as he fought to keep from breaking down. "Truth is, I ain't never had reason to feel jealous over anybody before. Ain't never had anybody I loved this much. If I lost you it would kill me, Brent, pure and simple." Jake took a deep breath then looked up at Brent for the first time since entering the room.

"That fella at the bar was right about something, Brent. I barely finished high school – only did because Ma insisted, else I would've dropped out. The only poetry I ever read is what's on greeting cards, and the only artwork

I ever look at are the comics in the Sunday paper. I really don't know why you took up with me in the first place, or why you love me. I only know that I love you more than life itself.

"Still, I never thought of myself as a stupid man, Brent, but now I think that it could be that I'm the *most* stupid man God ever set on this earth. I walked away from you. It doesn't get more stupid than that. Is it too late? Can you forgive me for being such a goddamn idiot?"

Brent walked up to Jake and put his arms around him. His chin trembled and his eyes misted as he crushed Jake to his chest. "Those did not sound like the words of a stupid man, Jake. Those sounded like the words of one of the most brilliant men I've ever been blessed to meet. You might not have a college education, but you're one of the wisest people I've ever known. Me, I have a degree, but you know what? I made an even worse mistake than you did. I *let* you walk away. We fit together, Jake, you and me, like two halves making a whole. That's why I love you. Of course, I forgive you, as long as you forgive me." He lost control then, his eyes overflowing and he leaned his forehead against Jake's shoulder for a moment as strong arms tightened around him. Brent could feel Jake's tears wet his shoulder, and felt his chest hitching.

Sensing a need to lighten the intensity of the moment, Brent said, "But I'll tell you something now, Texan. If you ever scare me like that again, I'll kick your ass all the way from here to Dallas."

Jake snorted through his tears, keeping his face buried in the crook of Brent's neck and his own arms locked like a vise around his back. "Oh, you will now, huh? City boy's gonna kick my ass?"

"I believe you once promised to bend over to make it easier for me."

Jake laughed, then lifted his head from Brent's shoulder and kissed him soundly. His hands slid up to cup Brent's face, holding it firmly between them as if he were afraid that should he let go, Brent would disappear.

Brent swiftly became lost in Jake's kiss, in his soft lips and warm tongue. His fingers un-buttoned Jake's shirt without Brent even real-izing they were doing so, then went to work on his belt buckle.

Jake's mouth left Brent's and moved on to his throat. His lips sucked fiercely on the ten-der skin they found there, intent on marking Brent with Jake's own brand. Brent's neck arched under Jake's lips, and he bit lightly at Jake's newly nude shoulder in retaliation.

Unbuckling Jake's belt and unzipping his pants, Brent slipped his hand into his jeans and underwear and pulled out his cock even as Jake's hand fumbled for Brent's own.

Standing chest to chest, their tongues met again as their hands stroked each other's

lengths into hardness. Each took the barest
moment to pull their pants down over their
hips, freeing their engorging erections in a
flurry of movement, too eager to touch one
another again to bother removing their pants
altogether. They moaned into one another's
mouths as their cocks became slick, their pel-
vises rocking together, hipbone brushing hipbone.

Brent sunk slowly down to his knees, pulling Jake down with him. He reclined on the
floor next to Jake, inverting himself so that his
head hovered over Jake's erection while keeping his own in easy reach of Jake's hot mouth.
The scent that was uniquely Jake filled his nostrils as he hungrily licked at Jake's cock,
groaning as Jake did the same to his own. He
slid his hand around a slim hip to cup Jake's
ass cheek in his palm, his fingers tickling at the
crack. Jake's fingers found Brent's balls, rolling the furred sac in his fingers as he continued
to slide his lips over Brent's cock.

Slurping loudly, the pace increased as they
devoured one another, thrusting into one another's mouth, and each taking in as much of
the other as he could. Brent bared his teeth and
drew them gently over the foreskin of Jake's
cock, as Jake swirled his tongue over the head
of his own.

Brent shuddered as he felt his orgasm rising, and pulled himself out of Jake's mouth.
Both men rose swiftly to their knees, facing

one another, panting, their hands a blur as they stroked themselves. Looking down between their bellies, they each grunted and watched as white ribbons of semen exploded over their fists between them.

The door to the office opened without warning, and Brent's secretary walked in, a stack of manila folders piled in her hands. It took her a moment to comprehend that she'd just walked in on her boss and his friend, both with their asses bared and cocks in hand, but from the high pitched, strangled squeak that she made it was clear to Brent and Jake that she'd figured it out.

"You might want to knock next time, Sherry," Brent muttered, neither man moving. In truth, neither one was capable of moving at the moment.

Another squeak and the crimson-faced secretary backed out, leaving a fan of manila folders and a snowfall of papers sifting to the floor behind her. They could hear her slamming drawers and heard the door bang shut behind her on her way out.

"Well," Brent said, calmly reaching into his pocket for a handkerchief and cleaning Jake's hand off with it, "I never liked her anyway."

Chapter Ten

"Ain't nothing for you to be afraid of, Brent," Jake said, as he sat astride his own red dun stallion. He had just helped Brent mount a docile gelding, a large horse the color of ripe hay and one that Jake knew to be gentle and possessed of a sweet disposition, but Brent still looked as though he were ready to spook. He was sitting in his brand-new Levis, cowboy boots, and brown Stetson, as still as a statue in one of the museums he used to drag Jake to back in New York, barely breathing. "He's not going to do anything you don't tell him to do."

"I don't think we speak the same language."

"You'll be fine. You just need to relax, Brent."

"He's too big, Jake. This thing should come equipped with a parachute," Brent replied, taking a quick peek down at the ground. He quickly screwed his eyes shut.

"I could get you a Shetland pony, if it would make you feel better," Jake teased, shaking his head at Brent. "Or maybe you'd be happier with a big dog." He stopped and eyed Brent when he failed to provoke a reaction from him. "Brent? Did you hear me?"

"Yes, I heard you. I'm considering it. Make that a medium-sized dog and you've got yourself a deal."

Jake chuckled, then clucked his tongue and gave his horse a small, gentle nudge with his boot heels. Brent's gelding plodded along obediently behind the more spirited stallion, its hooves clopping dully on the dirt.

"Jake? Jake!" Brent called, sitting as stiff as a board on the horse's back, afraid to move a muscle. "I think this might be a mistake, Jake!"

"Will you relax? You done said that you wanted to learn to ride. Well, I'm teaching you. Now relax, and try to enjoy yourself!" Jake called back over his shoulder. "You're perfectly safe."

"If it's so *safe* then why do you need the rifle?" Brent called out, gingerly holding the reins up in front of him his brow furrowed like he was trying desperately to remember everything Jake had told him to do. The gelding looked back over its shoulder and tossed Brent a patronizing look.

"I never go anywhere on the prairie without my 30/30. We've got diamondbacks out here. Although I might just shoot *you* if you don't stop flapping your gums."

***

For a short while they rode along in blissful silence, as the breeze rippled the tall grass in waves of gold and green. Brent had to admit that, when he wasn't sitting on the back of an equine brontosaurus, he was falling in love with the wide-open spaces and immense expanse of cerulean blue sky that was the Heartache Road Ranch. They'd named the ranch after the first bull Brent had watched Jake ride, and it had seemed a fitting name considering what they'd gone through to get there.

The ranch was everything Brent had imagined it would be. The low, rambling ranch house, constructed of stack chink dovetail logs and red cedar shingles, had a wide wraparound porch, four bedrooms, two baths, exposed beam ceilings, and the most impressive fieldstone fireplace Brent had ever seen. He smiled to himself as he remembered making love with Jake on a thick fur rug in front of a crackling fire on their first night in the ranch house.

Sprawled out on a semi-wooded section of their land, the house was set apart from the barns, corrals, bunkhouse and assorted outbuildings that comprised the working end of the ranch. It was rustic, barely more than primitive, and without any of the bells and whistles to which Brent was accustomed, yet it was feeling more like home than any other place he'd ever lived, and Brent was positive that the reason for that was Jake.

The only concession Brent had needed to

make to the layout of the ranch was the heli-
pad, a necessity in his view. He needed to
travel back and forth to Dallas for company
business, staying at the condo he'd purchased
while in the city, and counting the minutes until he could return to the ranch and his cowboy.
The helicopter made that return as timely as
humanly possible, shy of acquiring a jet.

Brent's attention was stolen from his mus-
ings by the gelding, who chose that moment to
toss its head and loudly blow air through its
nostrils, startling him. It sounded suspiciously
to Brent as if the horse were contemptuously
blowing raspberries at him.

"He keeps snorting, Jake."

"If I had a whiner like you on my back, I'd
snort, too."

"I think he just took a shit."

"They do that from time to time."

"That can't be normal, Jake."

"Trust me, it's normal."

"Good, because I think I might have just
done the same, Jake."

"Well, good for you. Your horse will feel
like you're one of the boys."

After an hour on horseback, Brent finally
began to relax, conceding that he hadn't fallen
off and broken his neck, and that it looked as
though he might actually survive the ride. After another half an hour, he felt braver and a bit
bored by their slow pace. He asked Jake to explain to him how to make the horse go faster.

Thirty minutes of trotting over the rough prairie had Brent cursing himself for having the biggest mouth west of the Mississippi. He felt as though his spine was getting ready to shoot out of his ass, and didn't hesitate to inform Jake of that fact, often and loudly.

Jake ignored Brent's complaints, heading on toward a stand of pine in the distance. When they reached it he dismounted, then walked over to Brent and helped him dismount as well. He leaned against Jake, his legs wobbling.

"That's it. I'm walking back," Brent said, rubbing his ass. "The only horse I'm ever going to ride again is a Mustang – the kind that comes with bucket seats and shocks."

Jake laughed as he tied the gelding's lead to a bush. "Stop your bellyaching and look around you. Do you know where we are, Brent? Do you recognize this place?" he asked, smiling.

Brent frowned and looked around, eyeing the trees and brush. He realized that he could hear the rush of a river nearby. "Is this… it is, isn't? This is where you brought me the night we first met."

Jake nodded. "I was pretty surprised when I found out where our ranch was situated. This is part of our land, now. I thought maybe you knew and had Josh buy it on purpose, but he said no. Didn't know anything about it. Funny how that worked out, huh?" He grinned at the shocked look on Brent's face. Walking a few paces further, he kicked at the remains of an old campfire. "Right here. Made love with you that very first time, right here."

"I remember. I don't think I'll ever forget it. Right beyond those bushes is the river where you tried to drown me," Brent laughed, ducking away as Jake tried to tackle him.

Jake chased Brent for a few paces then lunged, throwing his arms around Brent's knees and bringing him down to the ground. He crawled up over Brent's body, as he tried to wiggle away. Pinning Brent's arms up over his head, Jake lay flush on top of him, kissing him hard until Brent stilled beneath him and began kissing him back.

"Know what I got in my pack?" Jake asked a little breathlessly, tilting his head to nuzzle at Brent's throat.

"No, what?"

"I got us a pup tent, and a couple of sixes of LoneStar."

"What? No beef jerky?"

"You're being a smartass, ain't you?"

"Better than being a dumbass."

"You keep this up and I'll take you in for another swim."

"I'll be good, I promise," Brent laughed as Jake allowed him to sit up. He bent his knees, encircling them with his arms and leaned back against Jake's chest. "Man, I can't get over it. We *own* this spot, now? What's it called, Jake?

You never told me the name of that river."

"It's the Neches."

***

Spotting a curling plume of smoke rising a few miles or so up the west bank of the river, Billy Joe Flynt's thumb pushed the brim of his hat back further on his forehead. He'd been sitting on the grassy bank of the river for hours but hadn't had a single nibble on his line. His stomach was rumbling and even though he was sick to death of the taste of fish - having eaten bass and catfish more often than anything else since arriving at his daddy's cabin six months back - it was better than going hungry.

He'd made a few nighttime forays into town, usually aided by Reverend McGraw, but his supplies had run out again. Now he eyed the smoke as it lazily trailed upwards, wondering how many men were camped out on the opposite bank, and what supplies they had with them. Whatever those fishermen had, he decided, it would be better than the day-old catfish that Billy was looking at for supper.

Thinking about how hungry he was, and how pitiful the pickings were, reminded Billy of the reason he had sequestered himself at his father's fishing camp to begin with, and the thought of Jake Goodall left a bitter taste in his mouth that was far worse than the fish.

They should have killed that Brent Miller

faggot while he and his brother had had the
chance, Billy thought. Miller had recovered
from the beating they'd given him, Reverend
McGraw had told Billy during his first clan-
destine visit to town to get supplies, and he and
Jake Goodall had moved clear up to New York
City. Jake Goodall was living the high life,
while Billy Joe Flynt was eating catfish and
beans, forced to stay hidden from the law
along the banks of the Neches. His belly was
empty and he smelled like a sewer, but as bad
as it was for him, Billy thought, his brother
and father had it even worse. They were stuck
up in the Dallas County Jail awaiting trial for
attempted murder, among other charges. The
possibility of years in prison, maybe even for
life, was staring them both in the face.

He reeled in his line and picked up his
tackle box. Trotting back to his cabin, he
swiftly returned to the river with his shotgun.
Walking along the bank, keeping to the trees,
Billy headed downriver to a spot that he knew
would be shallow enough to cross on foot.
He'd cross the Neches, then circle back up to
the spot where he'd seen the campfire smoke.

If the fishermen were disinclined to share
their supper with him, then Billy's shotgun
would help them change their minds.

***

The sun was just beginning to set to the

west when Jake finished staking down the pup tent and building the fire. Unlike the first time he'd brought Brent out to the site, Jake made sure that this time he put Brent to work. He taught Brent how to pitch the pup tent, and instructed him on the fundamentals of building a fire, all of which Brent followed to the letter. After they'd seen to the horses, and had set Jake's pack, along with his 30/30 and two sixes of LoneStar beer, near the circle of river rocks in which the fire had been built, they were ready to relax.

"I feel like Daniel-fucking-Boone, Jake," Brent said happily, when he had first succeeded in catching a few small twigs aflame.

"Yeah? Well, I'd get you a coonskin cap, Brent, but you look better in a cowboy hat," Jake laughed, reaching over and tugging down the brim of Brent's hat over his eyes.

"Funny guy. Oh, did Josh tell you that the bucking machine is due to come in around mid-month? Where do you want it installed? In the barn?" Brent asked, twisting off the cap of a longneck. The two men were sitting close together, warmed by the flames of fire as the temperature dropped with the sun.

"Nah, how about the bedroom?" Jake teased, waiting for Brent to explode.

"Not unless you plan on fucking that machine as well as riding it."

"The only bull I plan on fuckin' is right here, and he's fixing to set his boot afire if he doesn't watch where he's sticking it," Jack replied, smacking Brent's leg and drawing his attention to the fact that the toe of Brent's boot was almost in the flames of the campfire. "The barn is fine, by the way."

"Good. Did you mail out your registration forms for the bull riding circuit?"

"Yeah, I did it this morning. Are you sure you want to spend all that money on a bucking machine and entry fees?" Jake asked, taking a long swig of his beer. "There ain't no guarantee that I'll win even enough money to pay for it, not to mention the expenses of being out on the road, you know. I told you I don't care if I ride the pros any more. I'm happy just being here, running the ranch."

"Oh, no, you don't. I know you better than that, cowboy. Besides, a deal is a deal, Jake Goodall. I promised to sponsor you, and you promised to ride. That was the deal. Don't tell me you want to welsh on me!" Brent cried, feigning indignation.

"I've never gone back on a deal in my life, Brent, and I ain't fixing to start now."

"Good, then it's settled."

Jake smiled, and finished off his beer. "I can't wait to get you on that bucking machine, darlin'," he said, winking at Brent. In addition to the beer, Jake had packed a cold supper for them, sandwiches of thickly sliced bread and rare roast beef, and much better, in Jake's opinion, than the dried jerky they'd shared on their first visit to the camp site. He unwrapped a sandwich and passed it to Brent, before taking one for himself.

Brent smiled at Jake's endearment. He'd taken to calling Brent *darlin'* and it warmed Brent's heart and tickled his groin each time he heard the drawled word. "Me, bouncing around on a bucking machine? Sweetheart, the only bucking I plan on *ever* doing is on *you*."

"Well, I suppose I can live with that," Jake laughed. He set his empty beer bottle down, wolfed his sandwich in three tremendous bites, and wiped his mouth on his sleeve. Letting out a long, drawn out belch, he grinned at Brent's resulting glare.

"I believe the only thing you've forgotten to do is scratch your balls, Jake," Brent said sarcastically.

"Ah, now, thanks for reminding me," Jake shot back without missing a beat, scratching his crotch vigorously. He snorted heartily at Brent's long-suffering look.

Standing up, Jake stretched and said, "I have to pee. That damn beer never has more than a passing acquaintance with my kidneys."

Brent smiled and watched him as Jake walked across the campsite and disappeared through the brush to the river.

***

Billy Joe Flynt looked up at the sky, at the

crimson that was slowly darkening into purple.
The sun was setting and he knew that it would
be full dark before long. He hurried his step,
although he still kept to the shadows of the tree
line. He was making his way along the riverbank when he heard someone step through the
brush about a hundred yards up from where he
stood. Freezing in his tracks he watched as a
man in a black Stetson approached the river
and pulled his dick out of his jeans, sighing
contentedly as he peed into the gentle water of
the Neches that lapped at the mossy bank.

Biting back a yelp of surprise, Billy recog-
nized the man. It was none other than Jake
Goodall, in the flesh. Fingering his shotgun,
which he held cradled in the crook of his elbow, Billy debated shooting Jake right there on
the spot. He smiled as he pictured the cowboy
falling face first into the river, dick still in
hand, and thought that it would be a fitting end
to the cocksucker.

Still, he hesitated, curious. Had that New
Yorker sent Jake packing back to Texas from
the Big Apple with his tail tucked between his
legs? Billy Joe thought that the possibility was
likely, and it tickled his fancy to think that
Jake Goodall had gone to hell and back for that
homo from New York, only to get trounced
out on his butt-fucked ass. Why, Jake might
even be eager to give that Miller boy up and
get a little bit of a payback. But even if not,
Billy thought, Jake Goodall was going to give

him the city faggot's address in New York. A
bullet or two to one or the other of his knee-
caps ought to loosen his tongue. And once
Billy had the information he needed, he'd put
another bullet right in the center of Jake's
forehead. That done, Billy Joe Flynt would
take a trip to New York City, all set to mix
some business with pleasure. He'd make it his
business to go, and shooting Brent Miller's
cock clean off of his body would be Billy's
pleasure. It sounded like a perfect plan to Billy
as he melted out of the brush and leveled his
shotgun at Jake.

For the millionth time, Billy Joe wondered
why Jake Goodall would want to sink his cock
into some man's ass. Jake was a fine looking
man and could have any woman in the county,
if he'd wanted them. Billy had never had too
much of a problem scoring pussy, but Jake was
another story. All Jake would have had to do
was flash that cockeyed grin at them, and the
girls would be bending over and flipping up
their skirts, begging him for it. From the size
of Jake's dick, which the cowboy was just giving a final shake, Billy Joe doubted if Jake
would leave any woman unsatisfied. A flash of
Jake Goodall, naked and pumping fast against
the softly rounded ass of a woman, flashed
through Billy Joe's mind and his own cock
stiffened as a result.

Without warning, Billy Joe's daydream
swiftly morphed from Jake riding a woman

into a vision of two men fucking hard. He could almost *feel* his cock slipping between Jake Goodall's cheeks. For the first time that he could remember, Billy Joe didn't push the daydream away in disgust. Standing right in front of him was an opportunity, he thought, and perhaps Billy Joe shouldn't act too rashly. Before shooting Jake, he might just indulge himself and find out for himself what it was like to fuck another man's asshole. See what the big draw was for Jake Goodall. After all, Jake would soon be deader than a doornail, Brent Miller's address tucked away securely into Billy Joe's memory, and no one would ever be the wiser.

***

Jake heard the crunching of leaves and twigs under foot and half turned, thinking Brent had followed him down to the riverbank. He opened his mouth to crack another joke about throwing Brent into the cold water of the river, when suddenly the stock of a shotgun came crashing down across his skull.

Crumpling to the ground, he could feel blood dripping down the side of his face from where his head had been hit. Dimly aware of someone fumbling at his waist with his belt buckle and pulling Jake's jeans and boxers down, he called out and struggled, trying to crawl away only to have his head cracked hard once more. He felt something hot and hard probe between his ass cheeks, and with a heave, succeeded in twisting his upper body around. A scowling face looked back at him, teeth bared, its angular features painted with shadows by the setting sun, and Jake moaned in anguish before succumbing to darkness.

***

"Hold still, you fucker!" Billy Joe Flynt growled as he whacked the side of Jake Goodall's skull with his fist. He'd already dropped the shotgun to the side, too anxious to rip Jake's pants off and have at him to worry about needing to shoot him. That would come in a few minutes, after Billy himself had come. And come hard, if Billy knew anything about the pressure that was already building in his balls.

He roughly ripped Jake's jeans and underwear down over the man's slender hips, exposing his firm ass, lightly dusted with dark brown hair, to the cooling night breeze and Billy Joe Flynt's eyes. Wasting no time, Billy Joe dropped his own jeans, then spread Jake's cheeks and aligned himself, ready to plunge himself in up to the hips.

A single shot rang out, shattering the silence of the early evening and flushing a small flock of birds from the neighboring trees. They took to the air in a flurry of beating wings and soft cries.

Billy Joe Flynt looked toward the spot where the shot had been fired, then slowly looked down at his chest. A small hole had appeared in the breast of Billy Joe's denim jacket, and the material surrounding it was quickly soaking up red. He touched it curiously with one finger before slowly falling face forward over Jake's body. Billy Joe twitched once and then lay still.

***

Brent dropped Jake's 30/30 and willed himself to move. It took a moment, but his feet finally obeyed and he dashed down to the edge of the river, skidding the last few feet on his knees. Reaching Jake's side, he roughly pushed Billy Joe Flynt's body off of Jake. The man's body was heavier than Brent would have thought it to be, but the rush of adrenaline that had hit him when he's realized what was happening to Jake at the riverbank gave Brent a surge of strength.

Gently turning the body of the man he loved over onto his back, Brent lifted Jake's head and tenderly cradled it on his lap.

"Jake? Jake?" Brent cried, brushing curls of Jake's sandy hair and clods of dirt away from his face. In the lengthening gloom of dusk, Brent could see that the right side of Jake's scalp was bleeding. "Jake!"

Fluttering open, Jake's blue eyes looked up blearily at Brent. "Get out of here, Brent," he whispered hoarsely. "It's Billy Joe Flynt! Get away now, before he sees you!"

"Never mind him. Are you okay? You're bleeding!"

Jake reached up and touched the side of his skull. "Ow, he said. "My head feels like a bull had danced on it. I've had worse. I'll be okay. Come on now, we have to get gone before he comes back. Help me up, I have to get to my rifle."

"I don't think he's coming back, Jake. I think I killed him," Brent replied, looking across Jake's chest toward the edge of the river, where Billy Joe Flynt lay as still as stone. He should feel terrified, Brent thought, but all he actually felt was relief that Jake was awake and speaking with him. He was still numb.

Jake's eyes followed Brent's line of vision, and widened at the sight of the body lying facedown in the mud, Flynt's pants still pulled down nearly to his knees. "You did that?"

"I heard you yell, Jake, and you never yell like that. I knew something was wrong, but I thought maybe it was a bear or something. Are there bears in Texas? I don't think it's safe for us to live here if there are bears here, Jake. I have to draw the line, you know? Snakes are bad enough, but I just couldn't tolerate bears…"

Brent was babbling as the reality of what he'd done sank in and ate through the shock. He'd killed a man in cold blood. "I'm a murderer, Jake."

"No, you're not. You saved my sorry hide, Brent. Knowing Billy Joe, he wasn't going to stop at just having at my ass. He'd have killed me for sure, Brent. I'm surprised he didn't shoot me first and fuck me later. He already tried to kill *you* once, remember?" Jake said, sitting up and pulling Brent into his arms.

"I picked up your rifle and ran down here. I saw him hit you as he was trying to rape you, Jake. It took me a minute to comprehend what he was going to do, but once I figured it out I didn't even stop to think anymore. I just pointed the damned thing and pulled the trigger. Oh God, Jake! The only gun I've ever shot was in a video arcade! I could've killed you instead!"

"You didn't, darlin'. You got exactly what you were aiming at. Now, just calm down and let's get back up to the camp. Probably won't get a signal on your cell phone out here, so we'll have to pack up and carry his worthless hide back to the ranch," Jake said, standing up and pulling up his jeans.

Jake stood over the body for a moment, looking down at it. He gave it a hard nudge with the toe of his boot, watching for any sign that the man still breathed. If he had, Brent was uncertain of what Jake would do, consid-

ering all that Billy Joe Flynt had done to them.
Brent hadn't missed the shotgun lying in the
grass, either. Billy had been armed, and Brent
had no doubt that the man had had every intention of putting a bullet in Jake's skull as well
as his dick in Jake's ass. Luckily, the body
didn't even twitch when his boot connected
with it.

Just to be safe, Brent squatted down and
felt for a pulse at Billy Joe's neck. He knew
immediately that Flynt was dead, because the
body was already starting to cool.

"He's about as dead as a body can get,"
Jake said. He stepped back over the body and
held out his hand for Brent, who sat trembling
and staring at Billy Joe's still form. "Come on
now, darlin'. We've got to go," he said softly,
helping Brent up.

"Jake, he tried to-"

"He didn't. What he tried to do don't make
no never mind," Jake replied. He cupped
Brent's chin and kissed him softly. "You saved
my life, city boy."

Brent rested his chin on Jake's shoulder,
looking down at the body of Billy Joe Flynt.
"He's one of the men who tried to kill me? I
never got a good look at him."

"Yes, darlin', it was him and his brother,
most likely under orders from his father. I always suspected that Billy Joe was gay, too.
Don't think *he* knew it, though. Don't think he
wanted to know it, which is where most of the

problems came in. I used to catch him staring at me sometimes with this funny look on his face. Like he didn't know if he wanted to kiss me or punch me in the jaw. What I know for a fact is that he was one mean, angry bastard, through and through."

"Rape is a crime of violence, so I guess it would make sense that he'd try to hurt you before killing you. It would have given him more satisfaction than if he'd simply shot you," Brent said thoughtfully.

Nodding his head in agreement, Jake led Brent back to the campsite, where they set about knocking down the fire and packing up their supplies.

Jake and Brent dismantled the pup tent and used the canvas to wrap the body up, securing it with the tent ropes then tying the ends of the ropes under the pummel of the gelding's saddle. Brent thought it was fitting that, in the end, Billy Joe Flynt would himself get dragged by a horse, and thought it most appropriate that the horse that dragged him be Brent's gelding.

The moon rose, painting the prairie in silver as the two men rode slowly across the plain heading back toward the ranch. Jake held a flashlight trained on the ground in front of them, its beam illuminating the grass, but the way back was still very slow going. By the time the outbuildings of the ranch rose in silhouette before them, it was the far side of the night and dawn was nearing.

Jake stored the body of Billy Joe Flynt, still wrapped in its canvas shroud, in a shed while Brent ran over to the guesthouse and banged frantically on the door, waking Josh Goodall. Josh ran outside in nothing but his skivvies, followed closely by his wife in her nightgown. Hearing a quick version of the story from Brent, Josh sprinted to the shed, Brent hot on his trail. First assuring himself that his baby brother was all right, Josh then went on to bark rapid-fire questions at him.

"What in the hell happened, Jake? What were you two doing out at this hour of the night? Ain't you got no sense whatsoever? You knew Billy Joe was still on the run! You're not going to be satisfied until one or the other or both of you is killed!" Josh grumbled, tipping Jake's head to get a better look at the nasty bruise on the side of Jake's skull.

"We went camping for the night, Josh, on our own land. Ain't nothing wrong with that. And how were we to know that Billy Joe would be stupid enough to be staying along the Neches? I figured he'd be down in Mexico long before now."

"Well, nobody ever accused the Flynt boys of being overly bright. Now you tell me exactly what happened out there, Jake," Josh ordered, as they closed the door of the shed and led the horses to the stable.

In halting words, Jake described the attack that had ended with Brent shooting Billy Joe.

He tried to spare Josh the details of Billy's attempted rape, but Josh would have none of it. "He tried to rape you? If he wasn't dead already, he sure as shit would be now!" Josh roared, turning a black glare at the shed. Then he turned back to his brother. "Brent shot him? One shot, dead center? I got to admit, I never would have thought that your city boy would've been handy with a rifle."

"He's not. I think it was luck, pure and simple. Probably could've hit me as easy as Billy Joe. But don't tell him I said that," Jake grinned as the two brothers handed the horses off to a couple of ranch hands who'd been awakened by the commotion.

"Best to call for the doc, Jake. You need to have that bump looked at," Josh said as they walked back toward the ranch house.

"Nah, I'm fine. Took worse knocks getting bucked off a bull," Jake replied, shaking his head. "Ain't nothing but a headache, is all."

"Somehow I don't think Brent is gonna be satisfied with that, Jake," Josh looked over at Brent, who had his arms crossed over his chest and was nodding. Josh laughed, throwing his arm around his baby brother's shoulders. "He worries worse than a mother hen about her only chick."

Once inside the ranch house, Brent immediately got on the phone with his lawyer. He'd called New York, awakening the man from a dead sleep. "Yes, the same one. Of course, I'm sure! How many men ever tried to kill me before? It was him. Yes, I shot him. No, I didn't have a choice, Bernie! He was trying to rape Jake. Should I have stopped and asked him for his identification first? No, I haven't called the sheriff yet. All right. Yes, okay." Brent replaced the receiver on the hook, looking up at Jake and Josh.

"Bernie's going to call the FBI. Billy Joe was wanted for a hate crime, he says, which is the FBI's jurisdiction, and Bernie doesn't trust the local sheriff."

"Neither do I," Jake agreed. "That man was purt near worthless during the investigation after the Flynt boys beat and dragged you. It was only after the news coverage got hot and the FBI got involved that he got to moving his lazy ass."

Brent sighed, nodding his head in agreement. He picked up the telephone receiver again, looking over at Josh. "What's the name of the local doctor?" he asked, ignoring Jake's frown.

"I don't need the doc, Brent," Jake said, placing his hand over Brent's and hanging up the telephone. "It ain't nothing but a bump on the noggin."

"Do *not* argue with me, Jake, or I'll shoot you, too," Brent said, scowling at him.

"Better listen to him, Jake. He doesn't look like he's playing, and I'll load the rifle for him, if it comes down to that," Josh said with a chuckle. He cringed comically at the look Jake shot him, then laughed all the way into the kitchen to help his wife get coffee on. "It's Doc Aldritch, over in West Fork," he called out as he disappeared into the kitchen. The kitchen door swung closed and the pillow Jake had chucked at his brother's back bounced harmlessly off it.

"It seems to me that you're outnumbered, Jake," Brent said, smiling. He picked up the receiver and dialed information, asking for Dr. Aldritch's number.

Jake shook his head resignedly, settling himself down on the sofa. After Brent had finished his phone call to the doctor, convincing the man to get up out of bed and travel to their ranch in the dead of night (which took some doing, even *with* Brent's silver tongue), he plopped himself down on the sofa next to Jake and leaned back into his arms. "Been a helluva night, Texan," he murmured.

"Truer words ain't never been spoken, darlin'."

"Will you promise to do me a favor from now on, Jake?" Brent asked, lifting his head from Jake's shoulder and kissing him tenderly on his scruffy jaw. "Next time you want to take me camping, promise me that we'll only pitch our tent in middle of a suite at the Dallas Sheraton, okay?"

Jake chuckled and kissed Brent's forehead. They remained that way, holding one another

close until the whir of the FBI chopper blades
reached their ears.

Chapter Eleven

Beauregard Sherman Thorken, dressed in a natty white linen suit (a favorite and the one that his mistress often told him made him favor Spencer Tracy in *Inherit the Wind)*, trotted up the steps of the Dallas Courthouse looking every bit the part of a fine, respectable Southern lawyer. A razor sharp part in his salt-and-pepper hair and a neatly trimmed goatee completed the illusion.

The fact that the entirety of B.S. Thorken, Esquire's practice was comprised of the defense of some of the lowest ranks of human garbage ever to be processed through the Dallas criminal justice system was not important. What was important, especially to B.S.'s two newest clients, was that his track record of wins was unparalleled. He'd managed to release to the streets a virtual parade of criminals, from rapists to drug dealers to arsonists, most of whom repeated their offenses and ended up right back where they started, sitting behind the defense table in court. In the circles that most of the more reputable lawyers of the city traveled, Thorken's office was known as the Pit Stop.

His strategy in the courtroom was a simple

one. Find a technicality and exploit it to the
fullest. If the prosecution's case was watertight
and sadly bereft of any technicalities, B.S.
Thorken was not above employing less savory
tactics to ensure his client's ultimate release by
creating a technicality himself.

Ethics was not a philosophy subscribed to
by Beauregard Sherman Thorken – unless it
suited him.

This case was perhaps one of the most important of his dubious career. His fee was triv-
ial in relation to the wealth of publicity the
case was garnering.

He had been hired by two local boys, Joseph Flynt and his son, Cody, to defend them
against allegations of assault and attempted
murder in the commission of a hate crime.
Cody, acting with his brother, Billy Joe, and
under orders from their father, Joseph, was
charged with beating a gay businessman and
dragging him behind a horse, nearly killing
him in the process.

The problem with the case, of course, was
that the businessman, one Brent Miller, had
survived. Had he died, B.S.'s job would have
been much easier. There was very little in the
way of physical evidence supporting the
prosecution's case. The District Attorney
really only had the testimony of a bartender
and a statement by the victim's gay lover's de-
ceased father. If it weren't for the victim's testimony, B.S. would have had his clients out six

months ago.

But, the case did have one saving grace, and one that B.S. intended to exploit to the fullest.

None other than Brent Miller, the victim, had shot one of the accused, Billy Joe Flynt, to death and it hadn't happened during the alleged attack. No, Mr. Miller had murdered Mr. Flynt in cold blood not six weeks ago along the banks of the Neches.

While Mr. Flynt, evidently, had been having sex with Mr. Miller's lover, Jake Goodall.

B.S. was confident that this latest turn of events would win his clients' acquittal. That Mr. Miller had not been charged in the shooting, and that the DA was confident that Flynt had been shot during the perpetration of an attempted rape, was irrelevant. As a matter of fact, B.S. had every intention of playing up the attempted rape to prove his point.

Billy Joe Flynt was a spurned lover of Jake Goodall's, and the entire beating and dragging incident had been a quarrel between Goodall's former lover and his new one that had sadly escalated into violence. It hadn't been planned at all.

Joseph and Cody Flynt had had nothing to do with it.

It was B.S.'s proposed strategy to draw out every sordid, distasteful sexual detail in this case, blow them up to billboard size and flaunt them over and over again in the faces of the jurors. His intention was simple: twist the facts so that Joseph and Cody Flynt were taken out of the equation, dazzle the jury with some fancy footwork and beat them over their pointy heads with the homosexual aspects of the case, and it would become simply an ugly dispute between lovers, one of whom was already dead.

He chuckled to himself as he recalled the embroidery that hung neatly framed on the wall in his den at home. *If you can't dazzle 'em with your brilliance, then baffle 'em with your bullshit.*

It was Beauregard Sherman Thorken's creed.

***

"Mr. Miller," B.S. said, his deep voice echoing in the courtroom, "You've testified that you had only just met Jake Goodall before you decided to leave with him to go camping near the Neches River. Is that correct, sir?"

B.S. Thorken was in perfect form that afternoon. He strutted across the floor in front of the witness stand, his thumbs tucked securely in his suspenders. His drawl thickened, and the expression on his face left no doubt about how he felt about the witness.

"Yes, that's correct," Brent answered. He'd been warned, had been told by the attorneys for the prosecution and by his own lawyers that the defense would most likely exploit that fact to try to discredit him. The oily bastard was up there doing his best *Matlock* impersonation and, Brent was sorry to say, seemed to be doing a bang-up job of exactly what his lawyers had warned him about.

"But-"

"You'd never met Mr. Goodall before that night?" B.S. interrupted, having got the answer he wanted from Brent, and not willing to allow the man to expand on it.

"No, but-"

"Yet you planned on having sex with Mr. Goodall that night, is that correct?" Again B.S. interrupted Brent, who was becoming flustered.

"It wasn't like that, I-"

"Then how was it, Mr. Miller? Were you two plannin' on goin' to church that night?" B.S. Thorken drawled, his voice dripping with sarcasm.

"Objection, Your Honor!" called one of Brent's lawyers.

"Sustained. Either rephrase the question, Mr. Thorken, or withdraw it, and refrain from the sarcasm, sir."

"Withdrawn, and my apologies to the court, Your Honor."

But the damage had been done, and B.S. couldn't have been happier. He gave the jury a look that spoke volumes about Brent Miller's

character. In those few short questions, he'd
managed to paint Brent as a slut who didn't
give a whit about who he slept with, and, by
inference, had insinuated the same about Jake.
He turned again to Brent.

"I assume that Jake Goodall gave you a list
of every man he'd ever carried on a affair with,
is that right?" B.S. asked Brent, turning to
glance at the first row behind the prosecution's
table, where Jake Goodall sat, scowling at him.

"Do you ask for a list of lovers before you
sleep with someone, Counselor?" Brent coun-
tered, quickly losing his patience with this
Colonel Sanders look-alike that was masquer-
ading as an attorney. He shot looks at the
prosecution attorneys, thinking that he'd have
a few choice words for them after the court
convened for the day.

"Your Honor," B.S. said in a long-
suffering voice, "Please instruct the witness to
simply answer the question."

"No, he did not," Brent answered before he
could be censured by the judge.

"Then you really have no idea whether
Jake Goodall had ever slept with Billy Joe
Flynt, do you?" Thorken asked, driving home
his point.

"He never slept with that bastard!" Brent
nearly shouted, indignant and furious that the
prosecution was sitting calmly by and allowing
Jake's reputation to be dragged through the
legal mud.

"Really? How can you be so sure?"

"He would have told me."

"Would he? Did you ever come right out and ask him?"

"Well… no, but I wouldn't had to ask. He would have told me!"

"Seems to me that if he was wantin' to be with you that night at the bar, it wouldn't have been prudent for him to mention that he had another lover, now would it, Mr. Miller?"

"Objection! Mr. Miller cannot testify as to Jake Goodall's intentions, Your Honor."

"Sustained."

"Tell me, Mr. Miller, did you get a good look at the men who beat you?" B.S. asked, trying a different tack.

"They hit me from behind. When I came to, it was dark, and my vision was blurry."

"I suppose we can take that for a 'no' then, is that right?"

"Yes, that's right."

"So you couldn't have picked the men who did this to you out a line up, now could you?"

"No, sir."

"I see. What was Billy Joe Flynt doing at the moment you shot him, Mr. Miller?"

"Objection!"

"Your honor, I am trying to show that Billy Joe Flynt and Jake Goodall had been carrying on a tempestuous affair. That Mr. Miller shot Billy Joe while he was engaged in having sex with Mr. Goodall is critical to -" B.S. began to explain, knowing he'd struck a nerve with Brent from the outrage that colored the man's face.

"He was raping him!" Brent cried from the stand, just as Jake rose to his feet, his fist balled at his sides. "That ain't the way it happened," he yelled.

The judge banged his gavel rapidly on the bench. "Sit down, Mr. Goodall. Another outburst like that and I will have you removed from this courtroom." He turned to Brent next. "Mr. Miller, kindly do *not* answer a question that the prosecution has objected to until I render my decision on whether or not to allow it!"

The judge had both sides approach the bench. He hemmed and hawed for a few moments, then nodded at Thorken. "Overruled. I'll allow it. Answer the question, Mr. Miller," the judge ordered.

"Billy Joe Miller was trying to rape Jake Goodall," Brent answered, his voice seething with anger.

"Mr. Goodall told you this before you shot Mr. Flynt?"

"No. Jake was unconscious."

"Ahh… I see. So you examined Mr. Goodall before shooting Mr. Flynt?"

"No, of course not, but I could see him."

"It was daylight?"

"No, it was evening."

"I see. So, it was dark."

"It was nearly dark. But I could still see

them."

"I'll just bet you could. Tell me, Mr. Miller, was Mr. Goodall struggling against Mr. Flynt?"

"I told you he was unconscious!"

"You said you hadn't examined him, Mr. Miller," Thorken interjected pompously, turning to look at the jury and shaking his grayed head.

"But-"

"The truth of the matter is that Jake Goodall was lying still for Billy Joe Flynt, isn't that right? And that you didn't know the man who was on top of him, but he did!"

"No!"

"No what? Mr. Goodall wasn't lying still? Or that you did indeed know who Billy Flynt was," B.S. asked, looking at Brent with a nearly comic look of surprise on his face.

"Jake was lying still, but-"

"No further questions for this witness, Your Honor," B.S. said, turning his back on Brent and returning to the defense table where Joe and Cody Miller sat, smirking.

In his closing arguments, Beauregard Sherman Thorken was completely in his element. He schmoozed the jury. He was their favorite uncle, the epitome of a gracious, old-fashioned southern gentleman, whose distaste for the subject matter of the trial was evident in his mannerisms. He didn't *want* to have to discuss the sordid facts of the case, in fact he *abhorred* being forced into a situation where he had, sadly, been given no choice. Two innocent men were on trial, brought there by the accusations of two homosexual men who had admitted - and quite clearly Thorken reminded the jury – to having few morals when it came to sex.

"Brent Miller was indeed beaten and dragged. The defense does not argue that fact, and indeed, feels badly that he suffered such an attack. However, the defendants were not the ones who attacked him.

"The prosecution has tried to tell us that it was Cody and Billy Joe Flynt who attacked Mr. Miller under orders of their father, Joe Flynt. That simply isn't the case.

"Mr. Goodall testified that he'd never slept with Billy Joe Flynt. By his own admission, Jake Goodall is a homosexual, who admits to having known Billy Joe Flynt, also a homosexual. By his own admission Jake had gone to the Lobo that night to pick up a man for the purposes of having sex. If you ask me, that doesn't really make him a man of character, now does it? Now folks, it's a known fact that Jake Goodall and Brent Miller live together out on a ranch purchased by Mr. Miller. We have established that Mr. Miller is extremely wealthy, and has purchased some very expensive equipment, such as a bucking machine, for Mr. Goodall's use. We've also established that Mr. Miller has paid for Mr. Goodall's entry fees into certain rodeo events, and that Mr. Goodall does not pay rent to Mr. Miller. Folks, who in their right mind would want to admit to having an affair with the man who beat up his meal ticket?

"We've shown that Brent Miller's testimony is as flawed as his character, ladies and gentlemen. He admitted allowing himself to be picked up at a bar by a cowboy he'd never met before for the sole purpose of having sex. More importantly, he admitted that he didn't get a good enough look at the men who beat him, and couldn't positively identify them. They could have been anybody, including his current lover, and he wouldn't have known the difference.

"Mr. Wells, the bartender from the Lobo tells us of a conversation he overheard between Joe Flynt and his two sons on the night of the attack. But it is our contention that Mr. Wells is simply looking for attention, and that his testimony is fabricated. Why else would he wait until after the news cameras started rolling to come forward with such a devastating story? Why else were there no other witnesses to this conversation in a bar as busy as the Lobo is on a Saturday night? If it happened after hours, as Mr. Wells contends, then why were the Flynt boys still there drinking at the bar?" B.S. said, pacing back and forth before the jury box. Every so often he'd stop and give a juror a sorrowful look. "It's unfortunate what some folks will do for a little attention.

"We heard testimony from Sheriff Wilkerson, who says that Ray Goodall, Jake Goodall's father, told him that Joe Flynt had paid Ray a visit and had insinuated that his boys had beaten Brent Miller, and might do the same to Jake Goodall. We couldn't hear that evidence from Mr. Ray Goodall himself because he, unfortunately, is dead. How convenient for the prosecution that we can't challenge his story.

"The ugly truth of the matter is, folks, that Jake Goodall and Billy Joe Flynt were lovers, and when Billy Joe found out that Jake was sleeping with Brent Miller he went on a rampage, beating and dragging Mr. Miller nearly to his death. That Billy Joe Flynt was one of the perpetrators is uncontested by this defense. What we do contest is that Cody Flynt and his father Joe Flynt had anything to do with it. We just don't know *who* was helping Billy Joe that night. For all we know, it could have been Jake Goodall himself!

"We do know that Brent Miller killed Billy Joe Flynt while Mr. Flynt was having sex with Jake Goodall. Now, Mr. Miller and Mr. Goodall contend that it was forced sex, and I must admit folks, that it certainly could have been the case. Mr. Flynt could have been so hurt and angry at Jake Goodall for taking up with Brent Miller that he'd tried to rape him. Or, it could just be that Mr. Goodall and Mr. Flynt had reconciled and it was Brent Miller's turn to fly into a rage. Either way, the only one who could have told us for certain which way the wind was blowing that night is Mr. Billy Joe Flynt. He is also the only one who could tell us who aided him in beating and dragging Brent Miller. And he is not here to testify today because Mr. Miller shot him dead.

"The only physical evidence that the prosecution could present during this trial is a coil of three strand yellow polypropylene rope found at the Flynt house, and a horse that belongs to Joe Flynt. Now, folks, I don't know about you, but I do believe that every ranch and farm all across the great state of Texas must have bales of that rope lying around, and I *know* for a fact that we have horses! The rope could have been the same that was used to tie Brent Miller to the horse, and that horse could very well be the same one that dragged Brent Miller, but it was Billy Joe Flynt who tied the knots and Billy Joe Flynt who was in the saddle. Who *helped* Billy Joe Flynt that night remains a mystery.

"The prosecution does *not* have any bloodstains. They do *not* have any fingerprints. They do *not* have any eyewitnesses. They do *not*, folks, have a case against my clients. Joe Flynt and Cody Flynt are innocent of any wrongdoing. The prosecution has failed in its case to provide any evidence whatsoever that proves otherwise.

"The defense rests, Your Honor."

***

The jury had been out for two days. Brent and Jake sat side-by-side on the sofa in the living room of the condominium Brent owned in downtown Dallas, both bare-chested, staring at a darkened television screen. Brent had turned the set off after the last dubious "expert" had given his opinion on the outcome of the Miller vs. Flynt case.

"They're going to walk, Jake. That slimy bastard got them off, I just know it!" Brent said, running a nervous hand through his hair. His fingers touched the bumpy surface of the scar that remained on the side of his head, covered by his neatly combed hair, and grimaced. "Scot-free, Jake. They're going to get off scot-fucking-free."

"No, they ain't," Jake said, slipping his arm around Brent's shoulders and pulling him in closer. "The jury ain't stupid. They ain't goin' to believe a word Thorken says. You mark my words, Brent. Joe and Cody Flynt's asses are going to be fresh meat for the boys over at Dallas Prison soon enough."

"You heard him. He twisted everything, Jake. Everything! He damned near had *me* believing that they were innocent!"

"I know he did. He turned what I said around, too. Shit, he turned what *everybody* said around," Jake agreed, then hugged Brent tighter. "You listen to me, darlin', it don't really matter whether they get convicted or not. Justice has a way of sneakin' up on bastards like that when they least expect it. Look at Billy Joe. He thought he was scot-free, too."

"What are you saying, Jake? You don't mean that if they get off we should shoot them! That's crazy!" Brent cried, sitting straight up and staring at Jake. He sighed and leaned back against his shoulder again, staring away at their reflections in night-blackened window, knowing that Jake wasn't serious. "I still have nightmares about the one I *did* shoot."

Jake chuckled. "No, that ain't what I meant – although it ain't a half bad idea, neither." He laughed at the shocked expression on Brent's face when his lover's head snapped back to look at him. "Relax, I'm just foolin' with you, darlin'. What I'm saying is that no matter how this thing ends, we are gonna get on with our lives and forget about them. We got the ranch and we got each other. That's all that matters."

Brent managed a smile, nodding his head. "Let karma worry about the Flynt boys, huh?"

"Yup. All *you* got to worry about is *me*."

"I do, huh? And what is it about you that I need to worry about?" Brent asked, laying his head against Jake's shoulder.

"Well, for starters, I got this little problem that needs looking after."

"Really? What problem is that?" Brent asked, suppressing a smile.

"This one right here," Jake answered. He took Brent's hand and laid it over the bulge at the crotch of his jeans. "See? Think maybe you can help me out?"

"I might be able to see my way clear," Brent answered, looking up into Jake's eyes as his hand began to rub Jake's cock through the worn denim of his jeans, feeling it harden under the material. "My, my… seems like your little problem is getting bigger by the minute."

"Best to take care of it afore it gets too big for you to handle."

"Well, we can't let *that* happen, now can we, cowboy?" Brent chuckled, as he unbuckled Jake's belt and unzipped his jeans.

Jake leaned back, draped his arms over the back of the sofa, and sighed contentedly as Brent bent over his lap and his warm, soft lips encircled Jake's cock.

"Lord, how I needed this," he whispered, his hand falling to stroke Brent's hair gently as he bent over his lap. Brent drew his length in deeply, his lips pulling gently, and Jake sighed again. "Ain't enough like this, though. Not this time." He pushed Brent up, forcing him to release his swollen cock.

Moving swiftly, Jake lifted his hips and shoved his jeans and jockeys down, kicking them to his ankles. He settled back again, his eyes darkening with lust. "Your turn, darlin'," he said, looking at Brent expectantly, his eyes shining with his growing desire. "I'm a-waitin'."

Brent licked his lips, tasting Jake on them. He trotted swiftly to their bedroom, returning a moment later with their standard equipment. Standing in front of Jake, he bit his bottom lip, looking from Jake to the lube and the condom that he held in his hand, and back to Jake again.

Brent knew that Jake knew what he was asking. He didn't ask often, usually being content to go along with Jake's way of thinking. But Brent needed him this time, maybe more than he'd ever had before. The stress of the trial was getting to him. It showed in the shadows beneath Brent's dark brown eyes, in the two small furrows that constantly creased the skin between his eyebrows, and in the worry that seemed to follow him like a shadow.

Leaning forward, Jake pulled down Brent's sweatpants and underwear, helping him step out of them. Brent's cock was at full mast, stiff and reddened, and Jake pulled it into his mouth for a few moments. He ran his hands over the firm muscles of Brent's calves and thighs, then up over his ass. After a few minutes of delivering sweet torture, his lips released Brent's length and he flicked his blue eyes up to meet Brent's dark ones.

Brent still held the lube and the condom, and he moved to hand them both to Jake, who made no move to take either from him, instead smiling his boyish, half-cocked grin and shaking his head. He rose from the sofa, kicked off his jeans and ran lightly into the bedroom, disappearing for a few moments, much to Brent's annoyance.

When Jake emerged from the bedroom, he was wearing his black Stetson, his brown leather chaps, and nothing else.

Grinning at the surprised look on Brent's face, Jake knelt on the floor, resting his chest on the red leather of the sofa cushions. He folded his arms and laid his head down. His knees moved apart, spreading his ass cheeks a bit and giving Brent a glimpse of pink puckered heaven.

Brent growled, a deep sound that came for his chest and opened the condom. A moment later Brent's fingers, coated with lube, prodding gently at Jake's asshole.

Brent bent over and began kissing Jake's back as he slipped a lubricated finger deeply into Jake's tight ass. He had always tried to respect Jake's preference, knowing how strongly he felt about playing the bottom. He tried to save such requests for when he needed Jake most, and this was one of those times. But when Jake had walked out of the bedroom in nothing but his hat and his chaps, Brent had nearly lost it.

He recalled thinking that the first time he'd seen Jake cowboyed-up, as the Texans referred to it, ready to ride a bull called Heartache Road, Brent had fantasized about fucking him in just this exact outfit. Wondering whether he'd ever mentioned it to Jake, or if he was just that tuned in to Brent's desires, he moaned, practically drooling. The sight of Jake's pale round ass framed in stark contrast by the dark brown leather of his chaps nearly had Brent coming without ever having to touch Jake.

As always on the rare occasions when he found himself allowed the pleasure of delving into the deliciously hot tightness of Jake's rear end, Brent found his own cock quickly engorged to nearly bursting and his patience with foreplay swiftly dwindling down to none. Now, faced with his ultimate fantasy, the longing to plow himself into Jake's ass became nearly overwhelming. Still, he fought his urge to bury himself between Jake's pale cheeks just long enough to spend at least a few minutes getting him ready.

One finger became two and two became three, slipping and twisting deeply into Jake's ass, his other arm wrapped around Jake's waist as his hand stroked his cock. He continued to lay kisses down along Jake's spine, then nipped lightly at the ivory flesh of his ass cheeks, leaving a trail of crimson marks rising to the surface of Jake's skin. Only when he had Jake writhing and wriggling against the leather of the couch did Brent finally allow himself the pleasure of removing his fingers and pushing himself past the ring of muscle that guarded Jake's body's most personal spot.

Brent's fingers slipped beneath the band of Jake's chaps, as he slid his cock deeply into the fiery hot, silky-smooth walls of Jake's channel. "Jake!" he groaned, "Oh God, Jake…"

"Ride me," was Jake's only answer, growled over his shoulder as he lifted his ass a bit and arched his back. It was exactly what Brent needed to hear at the moment.

Slamming his cock in to the root, Brent's pelvis slapped mercilessly against Jake's ass as he drove himself in to the hilt and withdrew, only to ram in once more. The pace he set was fast, hard and unrelenting, and his orgasm boiled up from his balls in record time. He spilled himself, but his frenzy didn't end with his climax.

Brent withdrew from Jake's ass, snarling, and roughly flipped him around so that Jake sat on the floor with his back to the sofa. Brent couldn't remember ever being this turned on before, so excited that even the shuddering climax he'd just achieved did not assuage his lust.

He virtually attacked Jake's cock, wrapping his fingers tightly around it and nearly swallowing him whole.

Jake fisted his fingers into Brent's thick

dark hair, nearly pulling it out by the roots as Brent's mouth sucked fiercely on his cock. His hips thrust upward as he fucked Brent's hot, wet mouth. Pulling out of Brent's mouth at the last possible moment, Jake allowed Brent to jerk him off, covering his lover's face with his come.

They lay back against the sofa, shoulders touching. As Jake's heartbeat and breathing returned to normal, he looked solemnly over at Brent, whose face was still smeared with the white trail of his semen. "It's the hat, ain't it? A body'd think you city boys ain't never seen a cowboy before."

Brent burst out laughing, then helped Jake stand up. He was still chuckling when they went into the bathroom to clean up.

While Brent was showering, he could hear Jake flick on the television set in the bedroom.

A minute later, Jake was sliding the glass door to the shower open. "The jury's in."

Chapter Twelve

Jake sat in his usual spot in the front row of seats directly behind Brent, who sat with the prosecutors at their table on the left hand side of the courtroom. He reached over and patted Brent's shoulder, knowing that the man was so nervous and wound up that he was practically jumping out of his skin.

Across the room, not twenty feet away at the defense table, Joe and Cody Flynt sat with their attorney, Beauregard Sherman Thorken. Although Thorken had chosen to wear his white linen suit, his clients were both dressed in conservative dark blue suits and starched white shirts, and both wore neatly Windsor-knotted ties. Clean-shaven and both sporting new haircuts, they looked like respectable businessmen rather than the scruffy, ill-mannered, hateful bags of shit that Jake knew them to be.

He frowned at the picture they presented, and prayed that the jury had been savvy enough to see through the portrait so carefully contrived by B.S. Thorken.

The bailiff, who entered the courtroom and stood near the Bench, interrupted his thoughts, and Jake rose to his feet along with the rest of those in the courtroom.

"All rise, please. Hear ye, hear ye, hear ye. All persons having anything to do before the Honorable, the Justice of the Dallas District Court now sitting in Dallas County, draw near. Give your attendance and you shall be heard. This court is in session."

As soon as the judge had entered and had taken his seat, the bailiff continued, "Please be seated."

"In the case of Miller vs. Joseph Flynt and Cody Flynt, the defendants are in court with their lawyer. The People are here, and the jury has indicated to the bailiff that they have reached verdicts in this case. We will be taking the verdicts in a moment," the judge said, looking from the defense table to the prosecution table. He noted that all interested parties were present, then nodded toward the bailiff. "All right, let's have the jury in."

Twelve men and women filed solemnly and quietly into the jury box, none looking anywhere other than at the Bench as they took their seats. The foreman alone remained standing, a dark-haired Hispanic man with a neatly trimmed mustache.

"The bailiff informs me that you have reached a verdict," the judge said to the foreman. "Is that correct?"

"Yes, Your Honor, we have."

The bailiff accepted the verdict from the

foreman, and looked it over, then handed it to the Court Clerk.

Joe and Cody Flynt rose to their feet, as did B.S. Thorken. All three had smug looks on their faces as they listened to the verdict being read. It was obvious to Jake and Brent that they had no fear that they would be convicted.

"We the jury in the above mentioned action find the defendants, Joseph Flynt and Cody Flynt, as follows: In the charge of attempted murder, not guilty."

The smug looks on Joe and Cody's faces, as well as Thorken's, morphed into wide grins, and all three shot a look of contempt toward the prosecution table.

Jake closed his eyes as the Clerk read the not guilty verdict, a tremor of anger running across his shoulders. He knew without being able to see his face that Brent was feeling the same fury at the verdict. He could feel the anger coming off Brent in waves.

"In the charge of having committed a hate crime, we the jury find the defendants, Joseph Flynt and Cody Flynt, guilty as charged."

Jake's breath burst from his chest, although he'd been unaware that he'd been holding it. Relief flooded his system, and he wanted nothing more than to lean forward and throw his arms around Brent.

Still, considering the circumstances, he kept his seat and his eyes trained on the Court Clerk.

"In the charge of aggravated assault and battery, we the jury find the defendants, Joseph Flynt and Cody Flynt, guilty as charged."

It was over.

The smugness on the Flynts faces evaporated in an instant, replaced in quick succession by confusion, indignation, and outrage as the Flynt father and son turned as one to their attorney. "What the fuck is this? You said we was getting' off, Thorken! You said nobody in the great state of Texas was goin' to take the words of a couple of faggots over ours! What the fuck did you do to us?" Joe Flynt bellowed.

Cody Flynt looked stricken, as if he were about to burst into tears, while Joe Flynt glared first at the jury and then at his lawyer, before turning his hate-filled eyes toward Brent. The ugliness coloring his face was a clear indication to the jury that they'd reached the correct decision in the case, and made more than one doubt whether or not he had indeed meant for his sons to kill Brent Miller. For a moment it had looked as though he were going murder his attorney, right there at the defense table.

The judge banged his gavel, calling for order. He set sentencing for a week down the road, then ordered the defendants remanded to the County Jail.

Brent and Jake watched as Joe and Cody Flynt were led from the courtroom in handcuffs and leg irons. Neither one could help the small smiles of satisfaction that graced their faces. The Flynts would not serve life, but they would both go away for quite a spell. Of course, there would be appeals, but none of that mattered to Brent and Jake. All that mattered was that the jury had seen through Thorken's web of lies and had found the Joe and Cody Flynt guilty of a hate crime and aggravated assault.

Justice had been served.

***

They were at Chase Field for the last go-rounds of the PBR finals. Brent sat in the front row of the stands just to the right of the first bucking chute, his fingers fiddling nervously with a small silver belt buckle embossed with a bull and rider. It was the buckle Jake had won the very first time Brent had watched him ride, nearly ten years ago. Brent never attended one of Jake's competitions without it.

Jake was thirty-five now, a senior citizen on the pro circuit, and had had returned to the circuit this year as one of the top ten riders in the country. He'd nearly won the Championship buckle the year before in Portland, Oregon on the back of a bull called Armageddon.

It was a ride Jake very nearly didn't walk away from.

Brent shuddered as he recalled watching Jake cling to the back of that black nightmare, twenty-two hundred pounds of muscle and as mean as a hornet's nest, bucking and twisting and snorting white streams of snot. Jake had made the whistle, achieving his highest score yet, a ninety-two. But he'd almost been killed before his score could be announced.

While he'd managed to stay on the bull for the entire eight seconds, Jake had been unable to loosen his bull rope so that he could dismount, and his hand had remained strapped to the bull's back. After another couple of seconds, the bull finally succeeded in bucking him off, but Jake's arm had still been trapped under the bull rope. The beast had continued to drag him along, jumping and bucking as Jake had desperately tried to disentangle himself while being shaken from side to side like a rag doll.

Finally, Jake had managed to free himself and fell onto the thick, reddish brown dirt of the arena, trying to roll away from the bull's stomping feet. He hadn't been fast enough, and had been freight-trained. Over two tons of bull had danced over him, leaving him with a dislocated shoulder, a concussion, a broken clavicle, three broken ribs, a fractured right ankle, and more contusions, cuts and abrasions than Brent could count.

Jake had spent the next two weeks in the hospital, followed by eight weeks in physical therapy. To Brent's amazement – and over his protests – as soon as Jake had arrived back home at their ranch he'd had gotten back on the bucking machine.

Jake's decision to return to the pro circuit for the next season had been the catalyst for one of the worst arguments the two men had ever had in their relationship. A cold war had been waged in silence for days, until finally, Brent could take no more.

"You've already nearly won the Championship, Jake! Why can't you let it go at that? We don't need the money! Do you have a fucking death wish? Is that it? Are you *trying* to get yourself killed?" Brent had shouted, as the argument came to a head and the two squared off, facing one another in the living room of the ranch. "Is it the buckle? We can buy you all the fancy fucking buckles you want!"

"When are you goin' to quit tryin' to be my mother, Brent? I'm a grown man and I make my own decisions! I'm a bull rider. You know that! You damn well *knew* that from the first five minutes we knew each other!" Jake bellowed back, slamming his fist down on the mantle of the fireplace.

"When I first met you, you weren't even quite twenty-five, Jake. You're thirty-five fucking years old now, and your body has been battered to hell and back. When are you going to grow up, Jake? You're too old to be riding bulls anymore!"

"You're fixin' to cross the line, Brent," Jake growled as he narrowed his eyes at the man he'd loved for the past ten years.

"I don't care. You listen to me, Jake Goodall. The doctors told you that if you keep riding you're going to end up in a wheelchair… or dead. I can't allow you to do that. I love you too much to stand by and watch you kill yourself!" Brent argued, trying to keep his voice level and not lose control again.

Jake looked at Brent closely. "Brent," he said, taking a deep breath to calm himself down, "*Almost* winning ain't the same *as* winning. I came so close last year that I could almost taste it! All these years of work, of getting hurt and getting right back on again, of sweatin' and swearin' and tryin' harder the next time out… what were they for? I need this, Brent. I need one more shot at the buckle. I swear to you, win or lose, this will be the last time."

"What would I do if I lost you?" Brent suddenly said, as his eyes misted over with frustration and fear. "Do you think it would be easier on me to have to bury a *Champion* bull rider than one who hadn't won the buckle?" He turned his back on Jake, unwilling to expose the depth of his fear.

"You ain't goin' to lose me. I ain't goin' nowhere without you. We got us a deal about that remember?" Jake said softly. He stood behind Brent, wrapping his arms around his waist and resting his chin on Brent's shoulder.

"Yeah, I remember," Brent whispered, folding his hands over his stomach, covering

Jake's with his own.

"One more shot, Brent. That's all I'm askin' of you."

"All right, Jake. One more shot."

Now Brent sat, a complete nervous wreck, as Jake strapped his hand down under his bull rope and pushed his pelvis up over his hand, finding his seat. Brent saw him nod, and the gate was flung open.

The bull was called Testosterone, and there couldn't have been a more apt name for the monster. It had balls the size of cantaloupes, and they weren't merely for decoration. In all the rides Brent had witnessed, this was the rankest bull he'd ever seen.

The bull didn't merely twist and buck. It flew, all four hooves leaving the ground in mighty leaps, its body twisting around and bucking in mid-air before crashing back down. Brent could almost swear that the behemoth shook the very ground of the arena when it landed.

Through it all, Jake kept his seat, his right arm swinging in masterful, controlled movements, helping him keep his balance. He kept his feet turned out and his thighs clamped tight over the bull's sides, even managing to spur the creature a bit, which added points to his score. His Stetson flew off, trampled beneath the bull's hooves, but he stayed on.

It was the best ride of his career.

Even his dismount was flawless. He landed

on his feet, running, scampering up the bucking chute wall while the cowboys on horseback lassoed Testosterone and managed to
drag the foam-dripping monster back into the
pens. As he clung to the top of the bucking
chute, his blue eyes met Brent's and suddenly
Brent had a vision of Jake, ten years younger,
grinning at him when he'd won the small
buckle Brent now held in his hand.

Jake's career as a bull rider was over, and
he was going out a world champion.

It had been a bumpy road from the start,
and Brent remembered how Jake had had to
hide who he was from the rest of the world for
so long. As it turned out, Jake's fellow riders
on the pro tour had known that Jake was gay,
had known that Brent was not his brother or
merely a friend, and it hadn't mattered to them
in the slightest.

There were always a few who'd had a
snide remark to make, and even one or two
who'd tried to use their fists to get their point
across, especially in the early days, but for the
most part he was admired by his colleagues for
his skill, his warm smile, and above all, for his
tenacity.

Epilogue

Brent stood before the curio cabinet that graced the wall adjacent to the fireplace in their ranch house, his fingers splayed against the cool glass. Within the cabinet, laid out in neat rows, were the spurs and buckles that Jake had won while he'd ridden in the pro circuit. Mounted to a plaque in the center of the top row was his Championship buckle.

Brent's eyes drifted down the rows to the smallest of the bunch, a silver buckle that was embossed with a bull and rider, and the one that held more meaning for both men than any of the other more prestigious awards.

For all of Brent's worrying, it had not been a bull that had finally taken Jake from him. The culprit had been much more insidious, and much more deadly. Diagnosed with cancer, Jake had fought it as only he could, as tenaciously and fearlessly as he had ridden his bulls, but as it turned out it was one ride he couldn't finish.

Tears fell freely as Brent opened the door to the cabinet and took out the small silver buckle, running his fingers over the embossed figures and remembering his cowboy.

"We had a lot of years together," Brent whispered in a strangled voice. "Not as many as some, not as many as I'd hoped, but all good ones, Jake. I miss you, cowboy." He clutched the old buckle to his chest, sinking down slowly to his knees.

In his mind Jake's gravelly voice answered, "*I ain't goin' nowhere without you, darlin'. We got ourselves a deal, remember?*"

"But you did!" Brent whispered back, his cheeks streaked with tears. "You left without me."

And again the ghost of Jake's voice spoke. "*I'm a-waiting.*"

The End

Printed in the United States
212903BV00001B/26/A

9 781934 166253